THE LOST DIARY

Dave Gustaveson

YWAM Publishing
A Ministry of Youth With A Mission
P.O. Box 55787, Seattle, WA 98155
(206) 771-1153

YWAM Publishing is the publishing ministry of Youth With A Mission. Youth With A Mission (YWAM) is an international missionary organization of Christians from many denominations dedicated to presenting Jesus Christ to this generation. To this end, YWAM has focused its efforts in three main areas: 1) Training and equipping believers for their part in fulfilling the Great Commission (Matthew 28:19). 2) Personal evangelism. 3) Mercy ministry (medical and relief work).

For a free catalog of books and materials write or call:

YWAM Publishing
P.O. Box 55787, Seattle, WA 98155
(206) 771-1153 or (800) 922-2143
e-mail address: 75701.2772 @ compuserve.com

The Lost Diary

Published by Youth With A Mission Publishing
P.O. Box 55787
Seattle, WA 98155

ISBN 0-927545-88-8

Printed in the United States of America.

To
Jan Rogers
for helping me
begin my exciting adventure
of writing to
kids.

Other

REEL KIDS
Adventures

The Missing Video
Mystery at Smokey Mountain
The Stolen Necklace
The Mysterious Case
The Amazon Stranger
The Dangerous Voyage
The Lost Diary
The Forbidden Road

Available at your local Christian bookstore or
YWAM Publishing
1(800) 922-2143

Acknowledgments

In Hawaii, I stared at the map in disbelief. Loren Cunningham had just finished detailing a trip he wanted me to take into Asia and Pacific with another friend. Having not traveled much at all, I was a bit overwhelmed. And afraid.

A few months later with thousands of flying miles under my belt, I was a changed person. After traveling into some of the neediest, poorest, darkest, and most unreached parts of the world, my heart was broken. My eyes had gazed into regions of the 10/40 window, an area presently targeted by Christians around the world.

This trip created a burden to see countless thousands journey into some of these same places. I trust your heart will become aflame with God's love as you read a book about this part of the world.

Special thanks to Mike and Rowena Burlow for their commitment to be missionaries to Turkey, and for very timely and helpful insights on Istanbul. Also to Max and Karen Hatfield for sharing from their visit there.

Thanks to Fred Markert for inspiration to write this book. Also, thanks to Jim and Judy Orred, Lori Gardner, and Mark Wilson for important contributions.

Thanks to Bill Pearson, Suzanne Howe, Nigel Burmester, and John Davidson for help along the way. And of course, to Shirley Walston, who edits with heart. And to Frank Ordaz, for a really great cover. And

I can't forget everyone at YWAM Publishing for their faithfulness.

And thanks to all the kids who keep me encouraged with stories of how these books have blessed them. To God be the Glory.

Table of Contents

Chapter 1

Running Scared

"**R**un!"

Jeff Caldwell's head swiveled in disbelief. His pulse quickened. His ears sharpened.

"Run for your life," the voice warned.

Jeff froze in terror and confusion. His wide blue eyes stared toward his frightened Turkish friend. Then he saw the angry group of bearded men running toward them. He felt like a quarterback—with an entire defensive line after him.

The warm surge in his veins quickly became a trembling in his heart. Adrenaline raced through his body, and he knew he had to move in a hurry.

"Let's go," the cry rang out.

Jeff shot up from the bench like a cannon, his bright purple shirt flying out of his jeans. Suddenly, he remembered his sister, Mindy.

"Sis! Let's get out of here."

Grabbing her by the hand, he jerked her along in stride and ran frantically to catch up to their Turkish friend, Kenan. The terror in Mindy's intense brown eyes seemed to fill her brown-rimmed glasses.

"Heeey!" she protested, but ran beside Jeff, step for step.

Jeff couldn't figure out what the problem was, but a sense of danger made him speed obediently behind Kenan. Kenan Mustaf, a Turkish businessman who owned a carpet shop, was housing their ten-day stay in Istanbul. Jeff trusted him to know best what to do.

Glancing at his sister, Jeff saw her quivering with the same fear he felt. He felt responsible for her. At thirteen, she was two years younger than him, and her legs weren't nearly as long as his. Mindy's blonde ponytail whipped from side to side as he pulled her along the way. With her mouth wide open, her braces sparkled in her tense, round face.

"What's wrong?" she cried, pulling free from Jeff's protective grip.

"I don't know," Jeff yelled over his shoulder. "But those guys are chasing us. Come on."

Jeff's thoughts scrambled as he followed Kenan through Laleli park. Glancing back, he saw the band of bearded men only a car length behind them. As big and angry as they were, Jeff was glad the men looked slightly older and out of shape.

Jeff's heart raced as furiously as his mind. It was

only Wednesday—just one day after their arrival in Istanbul, the capital of Turkey. Already, they were in danger.

For months, he had dreamed of shooting footage in one of the most historic cities in the world. Built on seven hills, it straddled the continents of Europe and Asia, a mixture of the modern and the ancient.

"How DO we...get mixed up in...things like this?" Mindy asked, beginning to sound winded.

"We'll talk later...keep running!"

Jeff felt grateful to be part of the Reel Kids Adventure Club, and he thought he knew why the club's journeys sometimes turned dangerous. Their leader, Warren Russell, head of their high school communications department, had told them that things going smoothly didn't always mean all was well. The club's summers and holidays were filled with purpose—and with that came adventure!

Deep in his own thoughts, Jeff scrambled through the park, always checking to make sure Mindy was close behind. He knew neither one of them could run much further.

Jeff, Mindy, and his best friend K.J., had traveled with Warren to this far-off land. Through the club, they had been to countries of the world most kids never had a chance to see—some, few kids had even heard about. The team had trekked up the Amazon River to a distant Indian tribe, sailed to Haiti, and even traveled through the African jungles.

Now the club was in Turkey to produce a video to inspire others, especially teenagers, to send out their own missions teams. The team liked to joke that even though the media club met "off campus," they were allowed to use school equipment. They met further off campus than any other club Jeff knew about!

Jeff and Mindy had joined the media club right after moving to Los Angeles. When Warren had first heard that their dad worked as an anchorman on a local television station and their mom worked part-time as a news correspondent, he'd kidded Jeff and Mindy that communications must run in their blood. Jeff thought maybe it did.

He'd looked forward to this trip to Asia for months, but not just because he loved communications. Centuries ago, Turkey was mainly Christian, but now Istanbul was home to only a handful of believers. The vast majority of people had never heard of Jesus. Jeff's team was in Turkey to try to change that. Like on all their trips, the club's mission was to reach as many people they could themselves, while producing a high-quality video to show others the needs of the people.

Remembering the mission, Jeff overcame the temptation to quit running. He glanced over his shoulder, wiping away the nervous sweat that ran from his damp, blonde hair onto his brow.

A ways back, one man stood with his hands on his knees and his head hanging down, gasping for breath. Another was falling away, but four showed no signs of giving up.

Jeff's heart skipped a beat, wondering if Kenan had found a hiding place. Any second now, the men could catch up. And Jeff still didn't know why these strangers were chasing them.

Even though it would have been comforting to have Warren with them now, Jeff was glad that he and K.J. were off filming in another part of the city. K.J. wasn't always aware of how much danger the club was in and had a knack for complicating things.

Checking the defensive line behind him again, Jeff saw the men slowing down. Finally, they skidded to a stop. Muttering in Turkish, they turned around and headed back the way they had come.

Jeff and Mindy slowed to a stop, watching to make sure the men had really given up the chase. Catching his breath, Jeff turned to see Kenan was resting several yards ahead. He scanned the crowd.

"I think..." Jeff began, "that Kenan was leading us into a crowded section of the park."

Mindy looked relieved. Then with fire in her eyes, she smacked Jeff in the arm. "Don't grab me like that again! Why did you yank me along? I feel like an old rag doll."

"Sorry. I just wasn't sure you could keep up."

"What in the world is going on?" she demanded, her face redder than her shirt, which was now crumpled and soaked with sweat.

Kenan made his way back to them. "Relax. They won't bother us now."

"Who won't bother us?" Mindy shouted in exasperation. "Who were those guys?"

Jeff waited for an answer almost as anxiously as Mindy. Looking into his Turkish friend's face, he saw the dark eyes flicker with excitement over their escape.

Kenan's dark, short hair and clean-shaven face made him look younger than twenty-seven. Always the professional, he was dressed in black slacks and a blue dress shirt that had been crisp before the chase. Jeff guessed some of his success as a businessman was his grasp of four languages—Armenian, Greek, Turkish and English.

Jeff wiped his brow. "Running in this July heat and humidity makes me wish I'd trained with the cross-country team."

Kenan's eyes moved back and forth across the crowd of people enjoying the park. Jeff's eyes seemed to follow.

"Got a little close, didn't they?" Kenan said casually.

"Who?" Mindy demanded. "Will someone please tell me what's going on?"

Kenan wiped the sweat from his eyes.

"They're from an organization called the Brotherhood. They're radical Muslims. Very radical."

"Why were they chasing us?" Jeff wondered. "We didn't do anything."

Kenan inhaled deeply, finally looking at his new friends. "They didn't like us talking to that Turkish man back there about God. They get violent when they find someone trying to convert a Muslim."

"How did they know what we were talking about?" Jeff asked.

"They must have seen us give the man that Gospel of John booklet."

Mindy looked horrified. "Then why did they quit chasing us?"

Kenan's eyes shone with pride as he pointed to the people all around them. "Because this area of the park is full of tourists. We get many visitors here, especially from Russia and Bulgaria. My people are very friendly. You'll love the Turkish people, especially their hospitality." Kenan smile faded. "Except the Brotherhood. They intimidate with fear."

"It's working," Mindy sighed and raised her eyebrows. "Will they hurt us?"

Kenan answered honestly. "If we hadn't run, they would have. We shouldn't have been in such an isolated section of the park."

"You mean we're safer in this crowd?" Jeff asked, jumping out of the path of a toddler on a trike.

"Yes," Kenan nodded. "Much safer."

"Then I'm staying here for the whole trip," Mindy announced, shuddering. "Right here."

Jeff batted at her ponytail, and Kenan laughed aloud. "You don't need to do that, Mindy."

"Why did we go there in the first place?" Mindy asked, calming down a bit.

"I'm sorry about that," Kenan apologized. "It looked pretty safe when we got there. A good place to share the Gospel."

"Yeah," Jeff said. "We were really starting to get through to that guy. I feel terrible that we had to leave."

Kenan understood how Jeff felt. "God is powerful, and He loves that man. Maybe He'll send others to talk with him, or maybe we'll run into him again. I took the chance because I hoped we wouldn't be watched. But the Brotherhood are very alert. They stop anyone they suspect is not Islamic—their goal is to get rid of every- one who isn't a Turk or a Muslim."

"Maybe we can go back later after they leave," Jeff suggested. "I'd really like to talk to that man again."

Mindy's eyes narrowed, and she nervously twisted her ponytail. "Over my dead body."

Kenan laughed. But Jeff knew Mindy was not amused.

"It's not that I don't want to talk to him," Mindy explained. "It's just that adjusting to this culture isn't as easy as I thought. It's hard enough to survive the maniac Turkish taxi drivers. And now this! A nice, rowdy California beach sounds good to me right now."

Jeff turned away, rolling his eyes. He knew his sister didn't really mean it. He just needed patience. He loved having Mindy travel with them, but she had a low tolerance for trouble sometimes.

Jeff took a deep breath, remembering how scared he had been himself during the chase. "Sis, it'll be okay. Kenan knows what to do."

Mindy shrugged and began chewing on a fingernail. "How long before we leave?"

Kenan checked his watch. "We need to find Warren and K.J. It's getting close to noon, so they can't be too far away. Didn't they say they'd meet us then?"

"Yeah," Jeff said. "I hope they got good footage. Do you think those Brotherhood guys will bother them?"

Kenan shook his head. "No. They're taking pictures—just like any other tourist. It's very acceptable. Because of our rich history, Istanbul is always full of visitors. Those men got so angry with us because we were handing out literature."

"Is that illegal?" Mindy asked weakly.

"No," Kenan replied. "In 1962, our constitution declared complete freedom of religion. But even with the law, there are two things that can get you in trouble here."

"Quick!" Jeff grinned. "Tell us what the other thing is before we do that too!"

"Obviously the first is giving Christian literature to a Muslim. Second, you can't say anything against anybody's religion."

Mindy was puzzled. "But you just said there was freedom of religion."

"That's what the law says. But the Brotherhood still

watch for those two things, especially if you're a Turk like me."

"What do you mean?" Jeff asked.

"I mean that being a committed Christian here means persecution. That's why there's only a handful of Turkish believers in the whole country."

"What kind of persecution?" Mindy said slowly.

"Some lose their jobs, their friends. Perhaps get beaten."

"What about you, Kenan?" Jeff asked.

"God has blessed my carpet business. Because I own the carpet store, I don't have to worry about being fired like some people do. But the Brotherhood sometimes make it tough on my wife, Parmelee, and me."

Kenan chose his next words carefully. "We sponsor a lot of teams who come here to share their faith. A number of them have been arrested, including me. Some were even asked to leave the country. I don't want to lie to you. It can get dangerous."

Mindy stepped back. "Oh great!" she exclaimed, throwing her hands in the air. "That's all we need."

Mindy clearly didn't want to continue the conversation any longer, and Jeff didn't blame her. Kenan had given them a lot to think about. They needed time to digest it.

The three of them stood silently for a few moments.

Suddenly, Jeff's face broke into a smile. "Look," he cried, pointing. "Here comes K.J. and Warren."

Jeff was happy to see them. He and K.J. had been best friends since the Caldwells moved to Baldwin Heights. Jeff shook his head. He watched K.J. in the distance, juggling his camera bags in one hand while combing his thick, dark hair with the other. K.J.'s hair was one thing he insisted on keeping neat—that and his camera bags.

Jeff's smile grew. He could see that along with his jeans and too-big t-shirt, K.J. wore his usual grin. It was good to see a friendly, familiar face.

K.J.'s ability to lighten up tense situations was one of the reasons Jeff liked his friend so much. A lot of energy was packed into his wiry frame, and even now, his friend walked with a familiar bounce.

Sometimes though, Jeff wished K.J. weren't quite so enthusiastic, or that he would have a better idea about when to cool it. Jeff was often left feeling like the straight man in a comedy team. *Somebody* had to keep his friend focused and out of trouble, and usually it fell to him. Even so, he had to admit he was very glad to see K.J. and Warren headed their way.

"Where have you guys been?" Jeff called.

"Around," K.J. shot back, tossing the bag that held his trusty Canon Hi-8 camcorder over his shoulder. He loved being the team's camera man, and he had proven that he was very talented at it.

Warren smiled, giving them a thumbs-up sign. He and K.J. must have had a good day. Before joining the club, Jeff and Mindy hadn't known any teachers outside of their classes. It had been hard to get used to calling Warren by his first name when they weren't at school. Now, Jeff smiled to himself, it was hard to remember to call him Mr. Russell when they were supposed to.

Dressed in dark brown slacks and a white sports shirt, Warren looked more like a teacher than Jeff and K.J. did. But sometimes, to the amusement of the team, he was mistaken for a student.

The team liked to tease their leader that his sandy

brown hair was so short he might be mistaken for an Army captain. Even when their joke got old, Warren still laughed.

His soft brown eyes radiated friendliness and warmth. Warren's deep love for God and compassion for people had made an impression on the whole team.

"Really, where were you?" Jeff asked again when Warren and K.J. had closed the distance between them.

K.J.'s dark eyes danced with excitement. "We went to an older part of the city. You wouldn't believe the footage we got! I got some excellent shots of these great old cars. It seems weird that they use old American cars as taxis here."

Jeff smiled. "You mean the dolmus."

"Yeah," K.J. said. "A lot of them. But I also saw one of those old panel trucks—a '49 Chevy, I think. I thought it'd be perfect for camping and hauling around our bikes!"

He looked around. All eyes were on him. "We could talk about that later," he told Jeff half-sheepishly. "Oh, and I filmed a couple of old Fords and Chryslers too. Can't wait to ride in one!"

The men chuckled while K.J. started to wind down. Mindy just shook her head. Jeff knew she hadn't appreciated the speedy taxi ride they had taken the day they arrived.

K.J.'s enthusiasm was contagious. "We filmed a Gypsy with some dancing bears," he continued. "It was so cool. And we got some footage of a mosque. Boy, I'd like to get inside there to film more."

Kenan shot a concerned smile at K.J. "We would really be in trouble. Big trouble."

K.J. and Warren both looked confused.

"What do you mean?" Warren asked. "Are we in some kind of trouble now?"

Jeff fidgeted. "Sorry, Warren. I've been waiting for K.J. to finish so we could tell you what happened."

For the next few minutes, Jeff and Kenan explained about the chase. Mindy kept glancing around.

K.J. interrupted. "Man, I always miss the fun stuff."

Mindy punched him in the arm. "Ha! You're usually the cause of it!"

"Ouch," K.J. moaned. "That hurt."

"Well, you wouldn't have thought it was fun if you'd seen those guys."

"Okay. Okay. But it does sound like great footage!" K.J. insisted.

Warren raised his hands to quiet everyone. "I think we're still pretty tired from the long plane trip. We've had enough adventure for one day. Let's head back to Kenan's house for food and rest. Is that okay, Kenan?"

K.J. piped in again. "I'm not tired at all, Warren. That flight was great. I couldn't believe we got to fly through Frankfurt, Germany. Those European flight attendants were really cute."

Mindy rolled her eyes. Kenan chuckled. "Let's go. We'll take the bus first, then the ferry. It will save time getting over the Bosphorus Bridge. There's always lots of traffic there."

"Just so we don't have to ride in a taxi or dolmus," Mindy groaned.

"I did promise K.J. we'd find a dolmus some time today," Kenan warned her. "But for now, let's catch a bus."

"Sounds good to me," she agreed.

The group headed out. Suddenly, Mindy gasped loudly, clapping her hands against the sides of her face.

"What is it, Mindy?" Jeff asked.

"My backpack!" she cried.

"What about it?" K.J. grunted.

"I left it back there…"

"Where?" Kenan asked.

Mindy turned pale. "By that stone wall. When those guys started chasing us."

Chapter 2

The Search

Stunned, everyone stared at each other. K.J.'s eyes widened. He shrugged. "Cool. I know what it looks like. I'll go back and find it."

"That's easy for you to say, K.J.," Jeff said a little louder than he intended. "You weren't there. Those guys mean business."

Silence hung in the air.

Finally, Jeff broke it. "We'd better forget your backpack, Mindy."

Warren looked concerned. "What was in it?"

Before Mindy could answer, a yellow taxi sped

toward them. Horns honked and tires screeched as the driver swerved to stop beside them. Kenan stuck his head in the front window and spoke to the Turkish driver, who muttered something, then raced away.

Kenan motioned everyone away from the street. "Let's go over here. Then the taxi drivers won't think we need a ride."

"Can you remember what was in your backpack?" Warren asked again.

Mindy rubbed her chin. Everyone waited.

"I took most everything out so it wouldn't be heavy." Mindy paused, then looked up. "Oh no," she wailed. "I had my good camera in there."

Jeff tried to reassure her. "We can buy you another camera."

Everyone smiled.

"I had some cookies..." she began. Then she stopped. Suddenly, the color seemed to drain out of her face.

"What's wrong?" Jeff questioned.

"My diary was in there too."

"Your diary?" K.J. muttered. "Why would you carry a diary around with you?"

Mindy took a deep breath and tried to ignore him.

K.J. leaned over, shaking one hand as if it were burned. "Boy, if the Turks find that diary, they'll have some interesting reading. I mean hot stuff."

Warren gave K.J. his Knock-it-off glance.

Mindy began to cry, putting her head in her hands.

"I'm sorry, Mindy," K.J. pleaded. "I was just kidding."

"I'm not crying 'cause of you," she replied weakly.

"What is it then?" Jeff asked, sliding his arm around his sister.

"I've really blown it this time," Mindy said softly. "Really bad."

Confused, Jeff knew something was really wrong. Everyone waited.

Mindy wiped her eyes and kept looking up at Jeff. "I had important names and addresses in it."

K.J. smirked, grinning wildly. "Is that what girls put in their diaries?"

Again, Mindy ignored him and turned to the others. "While I was researching for this trip, a man from our church gave me the names of some Christian friends here. I wrote their names and addresses in my diary. He warned me to be very careful. He said their families would be in jeopardy if people found out they were believers." She sniffled and looked up at Warren and Kenan. "I'm sorry. I thought my diary would be the safest place. I had no idea I would lose it."

Kenan's face turned serious. Very serious.

"What do we do now?" Jeff asked.

Warren turned to Kenan. Kenan thought for a moment. "We have no choice. We'll have to go back and find it."

Everyone stood still. Jeff didn't want to hear those words. And he didn't want to face the Brotherhood again.

But Kenan's mind was made up. "That man was right," he said. "If those names and addresses get into the wrong hands, it could mean trouble for those families."

"I'm sorry, you guys," Mindy cried, tears running down her cheeks. "We ran out of there so fast I forgot all about my backpack."

Jeff hugged his sister. "I should have grabbed it when I grabbed you."

Kenan clutched his hands together. "Maybe I'll go back alone," he said. "It'll be safer." He turned to Mindy.

"Can you tell me exactly where it was?"

Mindy was about to respond when Warren interrupted. "We won't let you go back alone. It's too dangerous. They won't bother us if we all go."

Slowly, Kenan nodded in agreement. "Maybe you're right. We'll be safer in a group. But we've got to get that diary."

Jeff was disappointed in Mindy. He knew she understood the danger of keeping names written in the wrong place. But as quickly as that thought came, Jeff tried to push it out of his mind. If he had learned anything in life, it was that he loved Mindy too much to build resentment against her.

Instead he thought about her vital role on the team. With her trusty computer and diligent notes, she was the team's researcher and writer. She always did an incredibly detailed job of preparing them for what they would face in other countries. Then after the team returned home, she wrote the script to accompany K.J.'s videos.

It was 1:30. The midday sun was blazing hot. Slowly, the team headed across the park. After they had walked awhile, Jeff stopped.

"Before we go any further," he said, "let's pray. God is bigger than those guys. He can protect us."

Everyone nodded. In that instant, Jeff felt very grateful that Warren let him lead the club. He realized that Warren tried hard to coach the team but let the team *play*.

Jeff lifted his eyes up to the sky. "Lord, You know we came here to show the love of Jesus to the Turkish people. Satan is trying to end our mission on the first day. But You're greater and You can protect us."

Everyone said amen in unison.

"We commit this time to You," Jeff continued. "Please protect the backpack and the diary until we get there. Amen."

Everyone looked up, and Mindy wiped the last of her tears from her eyes. As they left the crowded area of the park, Jeff looked toward the place where the chase had started. Fighting back great anxiety, he headed in that direction.

Walking slowly, he turned to Kenan. "I can't get something you said earlier out of my mind."

"What's that?" Kenan asked, curious.

"You said 99 percent of the people in Turkey believe in Islam and don't know Jesus."

"That's right. Perhaps 99.9 percent."

Jeff's heart filled with compassion for the people. "I understand Turkey was a center for Christianity for the first few hundred years of the early church."

Kenan nodded. "I don't know if you realize this, but this is where the apostle Paul preached the Gospel. This region was called Byzantium then, and when Paul talked about going to Asia Minor, he meant this area. It was here he felt he had finished his work of preaching."

"Wow," Jeff said. "What happened? How did we lose it?"

Mindy raised her hand, looking shy.

"I think Mindy has something to tell us," Kenan said.

"When I researched," Mindy said with a grin, "I realized the seven letters in the Book of Revelation were sent to cities in Turkey. Well, it wasn't Turkey then, but the cities are right here—Ephesus, Smyrna, you know. Even Antioch."

Kenan nodded. "Right. Antioch is where believers were first called Christians. Tarsus is in Turkey too. It was Apostle Paul's hometown."

Jeff had heard all this before, but it was just now sinking in. K.J. was listening carefully too.

With his mind whirling, Jeff turned to Kenan. "How could Paul see so many converts in this region? What happened to them? Now there are only a few Turkish believers in the whole country."

Kenan nodded sadly. "There's a lot more to the story than that."

Suddenly, the conversation was broken. The air felt tense. They realized they were very close to the place where the chase began.

Jeff stopped and scanned the area. The Turkish man they had been talking to was nowhere to be found. Benches were empty. This part of the park looked deserted.

Jeff relaxed a little, realizing that God had answered their prayer. Moving closer, he turned to Mindy. "Where'd you leave your backpack?"

Mindy pointed to a stone wall where she'd been sitting. "It was right at the base of the wall."

She headed closer with the team at her heels. Jeff's brow crinkled. He knew they needed to get the backpack, then get out in a hurry.

Mindy rushed over to the wall, then whirled around, a look of terror on her face. "It's gone."

Chapter 3

Surrounded

"Oh no," Jeff moaned. "What now?"

Kenan looked around cautiously. Beads of sweat dotted Jeff's forehead. A chill went through him.

"Maybe some kids found it," K.J. said, thinking positively. "Let's look around."

Mindy tried to hold back the hot tears pressing against her eyes.

Then Kenan's face changed, like he had an idea. "Mindy, was your name and address on the bag?" he asked.

Everyone turned toward her in unison.

"My home address was. I was afraid to put a Turkish address on it."

Kenan smiled. "Good. Let's hope a Turk found it. They'd give it to the police, contact your parents, and send it home."

"What if the police find those names in my diary?"

Kenan scratched his head. "That's okay too. They're too busy to go through the whole diary. But it would be bad if it got into the wrong hands."

"What if the Brotherhood found it?" Jeff asked.

"That's too scary to think about." Kenan bit his lower lip. "Do you mind if I ask what else was in the diary?"

Mindy blushed. She drew a couple of circles in the dirt with the toe of her shoe. Then she looked Kenan in the eye. "Personal things."

K.J. rolled his eyes and snickered.

Mindy ignored him. "I write out thoughts I have during my quiet times with the Lord. If anybody reads it, they'll know I love Jesus."

"That's neat, Mindy," Kenan said with a smile. "It's obvious you love Him a lot."

A blush rose to Mindy's cheeks.

Warren moved to stand near Kenan. "Maybe we should go to the police and report it missing?"

"Actually," Kenan said, "it might be better to wait a couple of days. We could call her parents to see if anyone reports finding it."

Just then, a chill tingled down Jeff's spine. His eyes were locked open. His heart seemed to jump in his chest, and his heartbeat quickened.

Coming out from behind a group of trees were six

or seven men. Jeff looked closer. Sure enough, he recognized their faces. They were the members of the Brotherhood who had chased them earlier.

Jeff glanced at Kenan for direction, but his friend looked shocked and confused, frozen in his steps. Mindy ducked behind Jeff and Warren. Jeff felt the chill grow stronger, beginning at the nape of his neck and creeping down his back. As the men grew closer, he could see an angry scowl on each of their faces.

Kenan let out a gasp. "Hold still. We can't go anywhere. They have us trapped against the wall."

The men stopped. Jeff watched a tall man with a full, black beard swagger toward them. His shaggy eyebrows, large nose, and wild beard would have been frightening on a small man. This man towered over Jeff.

Looking up into his eyes, Jeff saw rage. Angry passion. It was something he hadn't seen in other Turkish people.

With his heart drumming, Jeff whispered a quick prayer. He felt confused. Why hadn't God protected them?

The large man stopped right in front of Kenan. Jeff took a couple steps back. Although he couldn't understand the Turkish words, Jeff saw Kenan stand his ground as the man yelled in his face.

Seconds passed like hours. Helplessly, Jeff watched with the others. Then to his horror, the man turned toward him.

"My name is Abdullah," the stranger announced. "I'm a Muslim. Why did you come to our country?"

Jeff couldn't believe it. The man was speaking English. What was he supposed to say?

Gathering his thoughts, Jeff looked up. "We're visitors from America. We're traveling around Asia Minor putting a video together."

"Don't lie," Abdullah hissed. "We know why you're here. And we know your friend." He gestured angrily at Kenan. "He's a traitor to our cause and a troublemaker in our city."

Jeff stood still, not daring to speak. He hoped the man wouldn't notice his knees shaking.

For a moment, silence hung between them.

"It is against our holy law to speak against Islam," Abdullah finally said, "and to pass out your deceitful literature."

Jeff listened quietly. Then Kenan stepped forward. Instantly, two other men burst on him, shoving him to the ground. Jeff froze. Warren, K.J. and Mindy didn't move either.

Abdullah's face filled with disgust. "You Christians come over here with your false ideas and join people like Kenan. You foolishly try to convert our people. We'll make sure you don't do it again."

Jeff didn't even try to imagine what that meant. He glanced at Warren and waited. Silently. Afraid.

Casually, Warren stepped closer to Abdullah. Two more guys headed toward Warren but didn't touch him.

Warren stopped. "We're just a media club from Los Angeles, wanting to meet and talk with Turkish people. We travel worldwide."

"Don't make us laugh," Abdullah scoffed, looking again at Jeff. "We know your purpose. Your young friends gave part of the Bible to a man sitting over there."

Warren simply nodded. He wouldn't deny the truth.

Abdullah sneered, obviously enjoying the fact that he was in control. "There is only one God and his name is Allah. There is only one prophet. Mohammed is his name."

At these words, Jeff felt boldness drive away his fear. Feeling like David facing Goliath, he looked up at the towering man.

"Sir, we believe in God, too. He has changed our lives. We believe Jesus is the only true Prophet, the Son of God."

Abdullah laughed angrily. Then he smirked at Jeff. "You don't know what you're talking about. We know the kind of message you Americans preach. For hundreds of years we've watched you. First come your missionaries, then you send in your guns."

Jeff listened politely.

"You're no different than the crusaders of the past," Abdullah charged. "They massacred our people in the name of God. That's all we've known of your bloody religion. That's why we're at war with you. A holy war."

Jeff didn't want to hear the word war. "I thought there was freedom of religion here," he protested. "We understood Turkey passed a law making this possible."

Jeff wasn't moving, but his heart beat like he was running a marathon.

Abdullah laughed almost bitterly. "There is only one law here. The law of Islam. All other laws mean nothing. Even some of our own people allow for this law. But not us. That's why we call ourselves the Brotherhood. We are committed to getting rid of ideas like yours."

Abdullah looked back at the other men. They moved in closer.

"Give us your literature," he commanded the team, "or we'll have to take it. And that could be painful."

At that instant, Jeff remembered the diary. He hoped more than ever that they hadn't found it.

K.J. tightened his grip on his camera bag.

Immediately, Abdullah noticed. "What do you have in there, kid?" He asked roughly, moving closer to K.J.

K.J. stepped back. "Just some equipment, sir," he explained in a trembling voice. "Video equipment."

"Let me have it," Abdullah demanded.

As much as he loved his cameras, K.J. didn't even hesitate before handing him the bag.

Jeff had been trying to find a way to run for it, but he hadn't spotted any way out. Suddenly, his heart calmed. A few hundred feet away, he saw a group of policemen rushing in their direction.

Quietly, he let out a long sigh of relief. God had answered his prayers. Glancing at the others, he watched smiles break out on one face after another.

But Kenan wasn't smiling.

To Jeff's shock, Abdullah walked over to the policemen and greeted them like old friends. When he began pointing angrily at the team, Jeff began to understand. Abdullah was turning them in.

Everyone waited.

Warren looked over to Kenan. "What shall we do?"

Kenan looked at the angry men surrounding them, then turned to Warren. "Nothing. Let's hope we have a good policeman in charge."

"What do you mean?" Jeff whispered.

Kenan answered unhappily. "The police won't hurt us. But they might arrest us for passing out the Gospel of John."

Jeff shifted his weight from one foot to the other and back again. He looked at his watch out of nervous habit. Four o'clock. They hadn't even been in Istanbul twenty-four hours, and all this had happened.

Jeff felt the cold stares of the men. He didn't dare look at them.

Soon, four policemen strode up to them. An older officer with a large mustache turned to Kenan. Jeff listened carefully, but he couldn't understand a word of Turkish. He only knew that the policeman sounded angry.

Kenan turned to the team. "They want to search our stuff," he said flatly.

Jeff and the others opened their bags. The policeman shuffled through them one by one. Jeff was glad they had passed out all the literature—all except for a couple Gospel of John booklets in the bottom of his bag.

Stomping his foot in anger, the policeman threw these to the ground.

Jeff listened as loud words were exchanged in Turkish.

"What are they saying?" K. J. finally asked.

Kenan looked both worried and hopeful. "They might arrest us. Abdullah told them about the stuff we gave out. But the police captain seems to be a good man."

Jeff didn't understand. How could they be arrested in a nation that had freedom of religion?

Mindy looked at Jeff, and he knew she was remembering their conversation with Kenan after the chase. Kenan had been arrested before, and so had teams like theirs.

Everyone waited. The minutes dragged on. All Jeff

could do was pray and try to calm his racing mind. As he awaited their fate, he couldn't help but wonder what it must have been like here when Christianity flourished.

Jeff knew God had called the Reel Kids to Turkey. If only they could show these people that God wanted to reach them with His love.

The police captain yelled at Kenan again. Then grabbing Kenan by the arm, he herded the team away from the Brotherhood.

Abdullah laughed as he and his men walked toward the park entrance. "You haven't seen the end of me. If I were you, I would go home now."

Jeff tried not to react, but the words stung like a sword to his spirit. Maybe, he thought, they should leave.

Back in the more crowded area of the park, everyone stopped. The policeman had another conversation with Kenan. Then, to Jeff's amazement, all the policemen walked away.

Mindy gulped. "Those guys are not going to leave us alone, are they?"

Kenan smiled warmly. "We're safe now. They told us to stay out of the park and not to mess with those guys."

"What does that mean?" Warren asked.

"Abdullah will pass the word around Istanbul to be on the lookout for us. We'll have to be careful."

"What about my diary?" Mindy wondered.

"I told the police. They'll keep an eye out for it. Meanwhile, we need to get out of here."

"No problem with me," Mindy declared.

"Me neither," K.J. said.

The team followed Kenan to catch a bus. At the park entrance, Jeff noticed a man rushing toward them.

"Look," Jeff cried in surprise, as he saw him coming. "It's the guy we were talking to in the park—before the Brotherhood came."

Moving nervously, the man glanced from side to side before he stopped in front of Jeff. "Remember me?" he asked quietly in English. "My name is Kerim. I can't be seen here. After they came back from chasing you, the Brotherhood roughed me up."

Jeff's throat tightened. "We're sorry, sir. We didn't mean for you to be harmed."

"I'm okay," the man assured them. "But I need to tell you something."

The team glanced at one another, then focused their attention on Kerim. He looked so frightened, it was making them nervous.

"I saw a young boy pick up your backpack," he said finally. "He talked to the Brotherhood for a few minutes before he ran off. He looked like a street kid."

Jeff's mouth flew open.

Mindy gasped. "That means it's been stolen."

Chapter 4

Crash

The reality of those words hit everybody hard. Now they had to find the boy who took it.

"What did he look like?" Kenan asked.

Kerim looked around nervously. "I've seen him in the park before," he said, backing up. "He's short, but husky. He has a scar on his cheek, right side I think—easy to spot."

Kenan reached out to thank him as he hurried off.

Jeff wiped nervous sweat from his face. "Did you guys hear what I heard?"

"I think so," Mindy sighed. "What did you hear?"

"The boy spoke to the Brotherhood. They probably saw the diary."

"It's possible," Kenan agreed. "Let's pray the kid got frightened and ran."

"What if they saw it?" Mindy groaned. "They wouldn't hurt the families, would they?"

Kenan looked at her. "If they have the names, it'll mean trouble." He hesitated, deep in thought. "Mindy, can you remember what the names were? We should at least warn them."

Mindy yanked at her ponytail. "They were hard names I couldn't pronounce. But I think I have them in my computer files. I'll check my laptop when we get back to the house."

"Good," Kenan declared. "Let's pray for the best."

Mindy blinked hard to keep the tears away. "I'm really sorry. I blew it real bad."

Warren moved to her side, trying to comfort her. "Mindy, even if the Brotherhood found those names, God can protect them."

The others nodded in agreement.

"Let's get out of here," Kenan said, looking around. "Before those guys find us again."

As they waited on the busy street, Jeff noticed the buses racing by. Red, blue, and orange, they were all different colors and plastered with advertising decals. Gusts of black smoke poured from the older ones as they roared down the road.

Turning to K.J. and Mindy, Jeff overheard them arguing about taking a dolmus to the ferry. He knew

K.J. wanted to ride in one of the old cars that were used as taxis in Istanbul. But Mindy was nervous because of the reckless way the taxi drivers drove. He had an idea.

"K.J., how about taking one of these cool-looking buses over the Galata bridge to the ferry. Then when we get to the Asian side of Istanbul, we can take a dolmus the rest of the way."

When K.J. and Mindy nodded their agreement, Warren did too. Jeff appreciated the way he let the team solve their own problems rather than jumping in to referee right away.

Kenan rubbed his stomach. "My wife left dinner prepared for us at the house. I don't know about you, but I'm already starved!"

K.J. lifted his shirt and sucked in his stomach. "Look at this, I'm positively caved in," he said in mock horror.

Everyone laughed, and as they did, the stress of the day began to slip away.

It was just before six in the evening when the club arrived at the ferry station. The smell of fuel from the big ferry engines was thick in the air.

As they boarded, Jeff looked out over the huge Bosphorus Strait. Boats and ships of every description were backed up like cars at a busy toll way, waiting their turn to pass through to the Black Sea.

It had taken the team over an hour to get from the park to the ferry. Because Jeff and Kenan had planned the route that morning, he knew it would be another twenty minutes to cross and thirty more to catch a dolmus home.

Kenan led them into the inside lounge. Jeff scanned the passengers, looking for the Brotherhood.

"Why do those Brotherhood guys all have beards?" he asked Kenan.

"It shows their commitment to Islam. It's the mark of membership."

"Boy," Jeff said. "That Abdullah was pretty intense."

Kenan smiled. "You'll find this hard to believe, but he was a Christian once. Some people think he was faking it so he could spy on the Christian activity."

Jeff looked at Warren in disbelief.

Mindy gasped. "You mean he was a believer? What happened?"

"The church, which is made up of minority groups, didn't trust him. Most people don't think Turks can be converted. Abdullah got discouraged and angry at the people, then left the church. But the sad thing is he left the Lord too. Now he's full of bitterness and hate."

"I've seen that happen too often," Warren commented. "We forget that Christians aren't perfect. It's hard to keep our eyes on the Lord instead of on people."

"Why do people think Turks can't be converted, Kenan? You're a Turk and you were converted," Mindy reasoned.

"I sure was," Kenan exclaimed. "I used to hate Christians like Abdullah. I caused believers a lot of grief. Then I met my wife Parmelee."

"When will we get to meet her?" K.J. asked, as the ferry pushed away from the European side of Istanbul.

Kenan beamed. "She'll be home tomorrow. She's busy working with another team."

Jeff saw the grin on Mindy's face. "So how did you guys meet?" she asked shyly.

Kenan chuckled. "It's a long story. I'll share a little with you. Then Parmelee can finish it."

Curling her legs under her, Mindy settled in to listen.

Kenan's eyes sparkled as he began. "I'd probably still be a radical Muslim if it weren't for her. She's Armenian, which is a minority race in Turkey, like Greeks and Assyrians."

"Are minorities persecuted?" Warren asked.

Kenan nodded. "Around 1915, the first holocaust took place in Turkish Armenia, well before Nazi Germany. Hundreds of thousands of Armenians were killed by the Turks. Many were committed Christians. At that time, they had been winning thousands of Turkish people to the Lord."

Jeff and K.J. looked at each other in shock. Kenan went on soberly. "The Greeks and Assyrians weren't attacked like the Armenians. The Armenians were hated as fiercely as the Jews."

Kenan paused, reflecting for a moment. "If fact, the house we're staying in belonged to Parmelee's great-grandfather. It's an old mission house."

Mindy slid to the edge of her seat. "Kenan, this is exciting—a Turk marrying an Armenian. Tell us more."

"Well," Kenan continued, "there's much hatred between Turks and Armenians. Muslims hate Christians because of the Crusades. They took it out on the Armenians, who were massacred. Most Armenians don't think a Turk can become a Christian. They believe they're cursed." Kenan stared at the floor. "It's a miracle for me to be married to Parmelee."

"Wow," Mindy said, amazed. "I see that now. But how did it happen?"

"She worked next to my carpet shop. She'd come

over and visit. When I found out she was Armenian, I hated her. But as I watched her, I realized there was something different about her. It got to me."

"What was different?" K.J. chirped in.

"Even though I treated her terribly," Kenan explained, "she responded with kindness to me and my family. She treated me with respect and dignity. And of course, she is very pretty."

K.J. shook his head. "Yep. That'll get ya every time."

"So what happened?" Mindy interrupted.

Kenan's eyes filled with tears. "I couldn't fight it. I fell in love with her. Over time, she showed me the truth. She overcame all the things I was taught in school, like hating Christianity. We were taught that Christianity is a political idea destroying the world. She showed me that isn't true."

Kenan stopped to brush away the tears that spilled down his cheeks. "Parmelee showed me love, forgiveness and grace. My people had massacred her people, yet she loved me. That's the only answer to heal the hate between people."

Jeff jumped when the ferry thudded against the dock on the Asian side of the city.

"Here's where we get off," Kenan said, standing up. "I'll let Parmelee tell you the rest of our story."

Mindy was bursting with questions, but she nodded reluctantly and agreed to wait. The doors opened quickly and everyone hurried outside.

K.J. was the first one out on the street. He couldn't wait to get inside a dolmus. When he saw how madly everyone was driving his excitement only grew.

"What does dolmus mean, Kenan?" K.J. asked, bouncing in anticipation.

Kenan grinned at K.J.'s enthusiasm. "The word actually means stuffed, like a stuffed pepper. The drivers won't move until their cars are full of passengers. They travel fixed routes. We can catch one over there."

Kenan led the team in the direction he was pointing. Jeff watched cars career by and buses weave in and out of traffic. He turned to Kenan.

"Why does everybody drive so crazy here?"

Kenan laughed loudly. "Well, several reasons. First, these streets were created long before cars were invented. There are too many vehicles on the road. Everyone is in a big hurry. And just like in America, some drivers get crazy behind the wheel."

"Don't you have any traffic rules?" Warren asked.

Kenan gestured at the chaotic street in front of them. "We have highway rules, but no one follows them. Drivers do whatever they want at any second— pass, turn, speed or slow down. And the worst are taxi drivers. The dolmus drivers aren't that great either, but they're a little cheaper."

"Why are we riding one then?" Mindy complained.

Jeff held up his hand to silence her. "Remember, Mindy? We made a deal."

K.J. smiled smugly, then turned to Kenan. "How do they get these old cars to be so long? Do they weld two together?"

"No," Kenan replied. "A lot of people think that. But Ford, Chevrolet, and Chrysler made them especially for this part of the world. They have three seats instead of just a front and back like you're used to."

Kenan pointed to a green dolmus parked ahead of them.

K.J. ran to it, beside himself. "It's a '53 Chevy!" he

cried. "No, it says De Soto. I think they quit building De Sotos way before I was born. Look how long it is!"

"And crowded," Mindy groaned.

When Kenan gave the okay, Jeff, K.J. and Mindy hopped into the back seat. Warren found a window seat in the front, and Kenan squeezed into a spot with three Turkish ladies on the middle seat.

Up front, a large man almost smothered Warren. In the back, Jeff dripped from the heat and was afraid he'd choke on all the cigarette smoke. It seemed every Turk loved to smoke.

Kenan said something to the driver, who nodded, then roared into traffic. The heavy taxi swerved onto the busy highway, right into the path of a large bus.

Horns honked like a bad symphony. Jeff didn't dare look at Mindy. Finally, the screeching tire sounds stopped. Mindy was pale as a ghost.

"Already, that was too close for comfort," she shuddered. "And we haven't even gotten started."

Unfazed, K.J. raised his voice over the highway noise. "What kind of engine does this thing have?"

"A four cylinder," Kenan called over his shoulder, unable to turn around. "They used to have the old V-8s, but they replaced them. That's why they make this terrible noise."

Jeff felt like a sardine as they roared down the highway. Mindy's fingers dug into his right arm, and she hung onto the door handle with her other hand. Jeff didn't blame her. As he watched the cars race by, he remembered the Muslim philosophy he'd seen written on some of the large trucks—"Whatever Allah wills will be done."

That meant if you died, it was the will of Allah. Jeff

realized how insane this philosophy was. And how dangerous. It took all responsibility from people for acting sensibly.

Suddenly, Jeff tensed up. He sensed trouble. As the weight of the car shifted, it felt like the sides wanted to go different directions.

Veering to the right edge of the road to miss another car, the dolmus shifted even more. Watching from the rear seat, Jeff felt helpless. The driver pulled frantically at the wheel, but he couldn't bring the heavy vehicle under control.

Looking fearfully ahead, Jeff saw no way out. With another dolmus alongside them, their vehicle was being forced off the side of the road. They were rocketing downhill. Straight ahead was a roadside market full of people and their wares.

Jeff's mind raced wildly. To his right, Mindy's eyes were squeezed shut. To his left, K.J.'s were about to pop out of his head.

Jeff guessed they must be going sixty miles an hour. He heard Warren screaming up front.

"STOP! STOP!"

The driver appeared to be pushing on the brake, but the dolmus didn't even slow. The tents over the booths seemed to be coming at them like kites in a heavy wind.

Screams filled the dolmus. Seeing how scared the Turks were made Jeff even more afraid. As the people in the market scrambled to get out of the way, all he could do was whisper a prayer.

The other passengers were screaming at the driver, and he suddenly yanked at the wheel with all his might. The car began to spin.

To Jeff's amazement, the tires on the driver's side rose off the ground. For a second, they were riding on two wheels. Then, with an enormous crash, they thudded back to the cobblestone street.

"Yikes!" K.J. shouted, struggling to stay on the seat. "This is like a cop show on TV!"

But they were still headed for the outdoor market.

"Get down! Hold your heads. Quick!" Kenan yelled to the team.

Jeff couldn't tell the Turks' screams from his own anymore. He grabbed Mindy, pulled her close, then ducked. K.J. bent double over his camera bag.

SMASH. WHACK. BANG. The shriek of ripping metal overpowered their screams.

The front fender knocked down tents and poles, then something much more solid. Baskets sailed in every direction, and oranges splatted into the windshield. Carpets, crates and carrots were airborne.

Havoc and debris surrounded them. After the final thud, all motion stopped. The huge car's front fender had come to rest against a cement barrier, and the heavy car listed over onto one side, like a boat after a hurricane.

Inside the dolmus was one big pig pile. Like bowling pins in slow motion, everyone had been knocked into each other.

Dust filled the dolmus. For a minute, Jeff heard only the sound of passing cars and people screaming outside. Inside, everyone was shaken, too shocked to utter a word.

"Get off me, will ya!" Mindy finally said, breaking the silence.

The team untangled their arms and legs. Jeff scrambled out the side door, then reached back to give K.J.

and Mindy a hand. Kenan climbed out holding his head, and the team helped the Turkish women to safety, while the driver helped the large man out of his front-seat door. Everyone was shaken up, but they all seemed to be okay.

Jeff saw dust everywhere. Then he realized the dust wasn't dust at all, but smoke. The smell of it hit his nostrils.

Just then, Jeff heard a cry of pain from the front seat.

"It's Warren," Mindy cried.

"What's wrong?" Jeff pleaded, peering in through a broken window.

Warren looked up at him in agony. "I'm hurt."

Chapter 5

Istanbul

Jeff staggered, crying out to Kenan. "We've got to get him out of there before this thing catches on fire."

Before they could act, Jeff heard the loud noise. KABOOM. BANG.

Twisting in horror, Jeff saw flames shoot out from under the dolmus. He stepped to the front door, which was crumpled like an old test paper. Already, he could feel the heat. Panic gripped him.

Warren's moans grew louder.

Trembling, Jeff turned to Kenan. "We've got to get him out. This thing is going to explode."

Jeff yanked at the door. "It's stuck!" he cried. "I need help."

He heard Warren groan in pain. Mindy ran up to look at their leader through the windshield.

"Where do you hurt?" she shouted.

"My leg. I think it's broken," Warren moaned. "But don't worry about that. Just get me out of here."

"Hang on, Warren," K.J. hollered.

He put a shoulder to the car as if he could upright it by himself. A dozen bystanders came to help. They pushed and shoved, flames licking at their feet, until the huge dolmus fell back onto all four wheels. The tires still sat unevenly on crates and piles of vegetables, but they couldn't help that.

"Quick. We've got to pry the door open," Kenan commanded the driver.

The trembling man ran back, opened the trunk, and pulled out a tire iron. Jeff grabbed it, running back to the door.

The flames grew more intense. Jeff's shoelace caught on fire. He stomped it out and choked at the rising smoke.

He jerked at the door. It creaked like it had been rusted shut for years. It wouldn't budge.

Everyone waited.

Jeff clenched his teeth and gave it one last pull. With a loud pop, the door finally opened. Reaching in, Jeff and Kenan pulled Warren to safety. Now everyone was out.

Just then they heard another bang.

Boom. Boom. Boom.

Blazing flames engulfed the dolmus. Everyone fled from the ball of fire.

While Kenan and the dolmus driver talked to irate merchants, the team made Warren as comfortable as they could on a nearby carpet. Then they sat and talked to him.

Jeff let out a long sigh. "Thank God no one was killed," he said, reaching to pick up pieces of debris that littered the street. "We need to get help, but Kenan said ambulances are hard to get around here. Someone is trying to call."

"Well," K.J. said with a wry grin, "we certainly have a great story to tell about our ride in a dolmus, huh, Warren? Oh, if I only had it on tape!"

Mindy smacked him in the arm. But Warren only shook his head and chuckled.

The team took turns looking at Warren's leg and wincing. Jeff hoped it was only a bad bruise.

"Well, at least there aren't any bones sticking out," K.J. said positively.

Suddenly, a Turkish man screeched his car to a halt in front of the smoldering dolmus. He came running over. The man looked at Warren, then spoke to Kenan in Turkish. Kenan explained what had happened while the man poked and prodded at Warren's leg.

"This man works at the hospital," Kenan reported, when the stranger had finished his examination. "He'll take us there. We're not far away. He thinks the leg is broken."

Jeff's mind whirled. Things were happening so fast. This wild day seemed to have started about three weeks ago.

The team watched the man make a quick splint to

hold Warren's leg in place, then helped lift Warren slowly into the car. Jeff was glad Kenan was there to interpret.

As they sped to the hospital, Kenan sat in the back seat with Warren. Looking back, he could still see smoke rising from the dolmus.

"We're so blessed this man stopped," Kenan said. "This is what Turkish people are really like."

"I like Turkish people," Mindy said in a hushed tone. "But I do wish they'd slow down."

K.J. was quiet now. Jeff knew he felt like the crash was his fault because he wanted to ride in a dolmus. But Jeff didn't dare bring it up yet. He knew K.J. sometimes made jokes when he was afraid to admit something was bothering him. He could also tell Mindy was upset.

Jeff prayed as they moved through the busy traffic. Feeling calmer, he turned around to face Kenan. "What kind of hospital are we going to?"

Kenan smiled. "It's a private hospital just fifteen minutes northeast of the mission house."

Everyone breathed a sigh of relief.

"Until this man showed up," Kenan explained. "I thought we might have to go to the nearby government hospital. They can be pretty bad. But the one we're going to is the best in the area."

Just then the car went over a bump, and Warren cried out in pain.

"How much further?" Jeff asked worriedly.

"Another five minutes."

Jeff looked at his watch. It was almost eight o'clock. It had been the longest day of his life.

At last they pulled into the parking lot. Jeff studied Warren. He had heard Warren groan in pain, but never complain.

"I'm going to be fine," Warren stammered, trying to reassure the team. "Nothing is going to stop this mission."

"I'm sure glad we got you out of there," K.J. answered quietly. "And I hope your leg's just bruised or something."

The car stopped, and Kenan ran inside for help. Quickly, the Turkish medical staff wheeled a stretcher out and hurried Warren inside. The club thanked their driver, then ran to catch up.

In the waiting room, Jeff paced tensely. Kenan had gone to interpret for Warren, then find them something to eat. It was nearly ten o'clock, and Jeff felt like he hadn't eaten for days.

K.J. was still somber. Periodically, Mindy shot darts at him with her eyes. Jeff knew they needed to clear the air.

"We need to talk," Jeff began. "This accident wasn't anybody's fault."

A tear slid down K.J.'s cheek. "It's my fault. If I hadn't insisted on taking that dumb dolmus, this would have never happened. Warren could have been killed."

Mindy started to open her mouth, but Jeff raised his hand.

Kenan returned with some sandwiches and

slumped in a chair. "I think I know what you're talking about. Look you guys, if it's anyone's fault, it's mine. I decided it would be safe enough to take the dolmus. I take them often because the bus takes so long."

"Well," Mindy jumped in, "a bus is all I'm going to ride from now on."

K.J. smiled slightly. "That's okay with me. But accidents can happen anywhere, you know."

They stopped their discussion when the doctor came out.

"You can see him now," he said kindly, impressing them all with his English. "He has a broken leg, but he'll be fine. It's a miracle. From what I heard about his side of the dolmus, his leg should have been shattered. He's lucky it only broke in one place.

Your friend's in traction now. We can't put a cast on his leg until the swelling goes down. He can probably go home tomorrow afternoon. He won't be able to put any weight on the leg for a week. Then he'll need crutches."

Jeff was stunned. "A week. What's he going to do all that time?"

The doctor smiled. "Why don't you go ask him yourself?"

Jeff and Mindy hurried to his room. Kenan draped his arm over K.J.'s shoulder, and they followed behind. Entering Warren's room, they knew he had been through an ordeal.

Jeff walked slowly to the bed. Warren's leg was extended into the air, stretched tight.

"How ya doin'?" Jeff asked.

Warren forced a smile. "Still some pain, but better. Jeff, you're in charge now. Don't change the schedule for me. The Lord knew I needed a little rest."

Everyone smiled.

Kenan moved closer to the bed. "I'll pick you up tomorrow after I get my wife from the airport. Don't worry. I'll make sure the team stays on schedule. The important meetings aren't until next week anyway."

Warren squeezed Jeff's hand. "I know you'll do a great job."

Dawn broke Friday morning, sending pale streams of golden light through Jeff's bedroom window. Slowly, he awakened. When he tried to stretch, sore muscles in his back reminded him of the jolt of the accident.

He lay still, hardly believing all the things that had happened to them in one day's time.

Jeff reached for his Bible. Turning to his daily devotion, he shook his head in amazement. It was Acts 14, the story of Paul's preaching in Antioch and Galatia. They had just come over the Galata bridge the night before!

The words seemed to jump off the page as Jeff read. Derbe, Lystra, Antioch. These were Paul's mission fields, where Christianity had begun. Jeff couldn't believe the church had lost all that ground.

His thoughts were interrupted by a moan from K.J. Jeff couldn't wait to share this scripture.

"Listen to this," he said, tossing his pillow in K.J.'s direction.

Kenan lived in an old mission house located in

Moda, below the Bosphorus Bridge, on the Asian side of Istanbul. Bullet scars still marred the outside walls as a clear reminder of the persecution that had come against the Armenians.

After breakfast, the team toured the ancient stone building.

Their rooms were on the lower floor. In Jeff and K.J.'s, there was a cushioned ledge running around the wall that served as seating during the day and as beds at night.

Another downstairs room became a dining room when guests came. Along the walls stood ornately carved antique cabinets filled with an odd collection of dinnerware, china, and brassware. Photographs of family and previous teams adorned the simply painted walls.

Outside, a wooden balcony ran around one end of a small courtyard, and stairs led up from the courtyard to the living quarters. Kenan and his wife lived in two of these upper rooms.

The rooms were richly furnished with deep red, room-sized carpets and dark blue curtains and cushion covers. It was obvious to Jeff that Kenan was in the carpet business. Otherwise, it would have been too expensive to furnish his house.

Jeff was grateful to be staying there. He thought of the history of the old mission house and wondered how many prayer meetings had taken place under its red tile roof.

After visiting Warren, Jeff and the others bounced along in an old Turkish bus.

"Does this feel safer, Mindy?" Jeff teased.

Mindy smiled and stretched one arm over her head. "Yeah, but I'm a little sore. Must be from the crash."

Everyone nodded in unison. They were all sore.

Mindy leaned forward to speak to K.J. "I'm sorry about last night. I had no right to blame you."

K.J. shrugged his wiry shoulders.

"Would you forgive me, K.J.?" Mindy asked softly.

K.J. grinned at her and nodded.

Jeff was proud of his sister. He knew she would come through. She always did. That's what the Reel Kids Adventure Club was all about—living out principles in God's Word in the midst of life's trials and adventures. Jeff knew the club would have some conflict, but forgiveness and love always moved them beyond it.

Everyone sat in peaceful silence.

"I'm excited about today," Jeff finally said. "I've looked forward to seeing Istanbul for a long time."

"Do you know much about it?" Kenan asked.

Jeff started to answer, when Mindy held up a finger.

"I can tell you a few things," she said with a satisfied smile.

Kenan nodded in approval. K.J. grinned as if he knew this had been coming.

Reaching into a bag, Mindy pulled out a notebook with several pages of neat, computer-typed notes. "Here's what I have. Istanbul is one of the four great cities of the world. It ranks with Athens, Rome and Jerusalem because of its influence on our thoughts and way of life."

Kenan grinned.

Mindy went on. "Had it not been for Constantinople—which is now called Istanbul, we would have no Roman law, very little Greek art, and the history of Christianity might be very different."

Jeff was proud of his sister for her detailed research.

K.J. looked impressed. "Go, Mindy. You're on a roll."

"Well," Mindy beamed, "lots of stuff makes this place a city of amazing importance: the lay of the land, the climate, and the location of the three waterways."

"You're right," K.J. exclaimed. "This place has water all around. It's like a natural fortress."

Mindy loved her role as teacher. As the bus bounced along, she read more from her notes. Then she pulled out a map of Istanbul and pointed.

"Look. The city is a triangle bounded on two sides by water. To the northwest, the Black Sea and the long, curved harbor of the famous Golden Horn. To the southwest, the Sea of Marmara. And between the two, the Sea of Bosphorus flows swiftly from the north."

K.J. jumped in. "I can't wait to shoot some of this. This is going to be an incredible video."

Suddenly, Jeff pointed straight ahead. "Look. We're heading across the Bosphorus again. It separates the Asian and European sides of the city, right? See those ships? They're coming from the Black Sea."

"It looks like a flooded L.A. freeway out there," K.J. moaned. "This traffic does take time."

Everyone stopped talking to take in the sights. K.J. pulled out his video camera while Jeff watched the jumble of domes and minarets, towers and palaces, hotels and offices.

"Istanbul is built on seven hills," Mindy continued. "We should be able to see them soon."

Jeff spotted a large statue to his left. "What's that, Mindy?"

She looked toward Kenan and shrugged.

"That's a statue of Attaturk," Kenan explained. "He's the father of modern Turkey. You'll see his bust everywhere—with the inscription 'Happy is he who can say he is a Turk.'"

"Well, I read about him," Mindy said in self-defense, "but I didn't know that was his statue."

Jeff craned his head all around to view the busy Bosphorus Sea.

Suddenly, he felt someone watching him. He swiveled in his seat, scanning the passengers until his eyes locked on a man at the back of the bus. Jeff reached up to his face, almost expecting it to be scorched from the intensity of the man's gaze.

His heart sank. The man had a shaggy, black beard.

Chapter 6

✦ ✦ ✦ ✦ ✦

Sancta Sophia

Jeff whirled around. He wanted to tell Kenan, but he was frozen in fear.

After a few deep breaths, he leaned close to Kenan. "Don't look now," he whispered, "but I think one of the Brotherhood is on the bus. He's staring at us."

He gulped as Kenan immediately turned to look. To his horror, Kenan got up and walked back to the stranger. *What could he be thinking?*

After a few moments, Jeff dared to look. The two men were laughing together. Shaking his head in confusion, Jeff rolled his shoulders to loosen the tension.

Soon Kenan returned, grinning mischievously.

"How'd you get that Brotherhood man to laugh with you?" Jeff stammered.

Kenan laughed. "Jeff, every bearded man in Istanbul is not part of the Brotherhood. That guy is simply riding the bus to work. He was curious about you guys. I had a good time sharing with him about the Gospel."

Jeff let out a gasp of relief. "Oh. Well, we'd better get that diary back or we'll see lots of bearded men who *are* part of the Brotherhood."

Kenan was still chuckling. "We're getting closer to the important historic sights," he said, pointing toward the land. "This is one of my favorite areas because it's where the waterways meet."

The bus crawled to a stop just past the Galata Bridge.

"Are we getting off?" Jeff asked.

Kenan nodded. "We need to catch another bus. Remember, traveling takes a bit longer on the bus."

"Maybe we should take a dolmus," K.J. suggested cheerfully, grinning at Mindy.

This time, Mindy smiled back.

As they waited on a bench, Kenan turned to the team. "Tell me more about the video you're producing."

K.J.'s face lit up. He picked up his camera and zeroed in on Kenan's face. "Our goal is to inform people back home about the 10/40 window. I'm sure you've noticed this camera attached to my face."

"Isn't the 10/40 window a bit hard to explain?" Kenan wondered.

"Hang on, hang on," K.J. said, stepping back to plan the shot. "Let's make this an interview. Jeff, scoot over closer, then explain it to him. Pretend he's never heard of it."

Jeff cleared his throat and spouted a line he'd memorized. "The 10/40 window is the specific geographical area where most of the world's poorest and least evangelized people live."

Flustered, he began to explain it in his own words.

"The area is called a window because if you draw it on a world map, that's how it's shaped—rectangular, like a window. Let's pretend we have a map here," he said, grabbing a piece of paper and a pen from Mindy's hand.

"We draw two lines across the world—one at ten degrees north of the equator and one at forty degrees north. Now we connect the ends of the lines. What we have is a window that extends across West Africa and Asia. Only one-third of the world's land is in that area, but the sixty-two nations in the middle contain two-thirds of the world's total population."

"Wow!" K.J. exclaimed, letting his camera slip. "I didn't know that."

"Adam and Eve lived in this area," Jeff said. "Their sin allowed Satan to get control of the earth."

Jeff could tell Mindy wanted to jump in. She held her notes in the air.

"What amazed me," she said, "is that eight out of ten of the world's poorest of the poor live in this window. Their quality of life is horrible. It's the worst place for early deaths, especially among infants. And it has the greatest percentage of people who can't read."

Kenan nodded and looked into her eyes. "Mindy,

now you know why I live in Istanbul. It has been a strategic center for this area for hundreds of years."

Just then, the bus pulled up. Hastily, the team shoved their things into their bags and hopped on.

"Okay," Kenan said. "In about ten minutes, we'll be at a church completed in the year 548. For a thousand years, it reigned as the greatest church in the world. You've probably heard of *Sancta Sophia,* but we Turks say *Aya Sophia.* Sophia was not a saint. The word means *wisdom.*"

In a few minutes, the bus jerked to a stop in front of an enormous pale rose structure. Jeff had never seen anything like it. All around, supports, kiosks and out-buildings hugged the church's massive walls.

Jeff's eyes widened when he saw the enormous dome and stone minarets. Below the dome was an arched entrance that looked large enough to hold an inflated hot air balloon.

"How big is that dome?" Jeff asked as they walked to the main entrance and paid their five-dollar entrance fees.

"About 180 feet tall," Kenan answered, then directed them to a flight of stone steps. "Here are the sunken ruins of an early sixth-century Theodosian church. You're walking down the original steps."

Jeff paused in awe. K.J. took them two at a time so he could film the team walking down.

They entered the church slowly, one step at a time. The darkness was broken by brilliant colors that flooded through stained glass windows. Two massive doorways appeared. Far beyond them, in the dim light, stood another semi-dome blazing with gold mosaics portraying the Madonna and Child.

Everywhere Jeff looked, he was awestruck. Mindy's mouth never closed. The stonework was breathtaking, not to mention the colossal columns of purple and dark green marble.

In reverent silence, Jeff and the team walked through the church. Beautiful mosaics surprised them around every corner, telling stories with colors and design. Most impressive were the mosaics of Christ.

"I can't believe this church was ever turned into a mosque," Jeff said, as they climbed back up the stone stairs.

Kenan smiled. "Many mosaics were plastered over when Istanbul was captured in 1453. Now Aya Sophia's being refurbished as a museum. Justinian built it in the sixth century, thinking he had surpassed Solomon's wealth and wisdom."

"In fact," Kenan told the team, "the size was so awesome that when Constantine's subjects came from distant parts of the country, where buildings were not much taller than their heads, they thought they were entering the Kingdom of God."

"I've seen lots of high-rises," Mindy said, "but I can understand why they thought that. This architecture is incredible! That dome seems to have nothing holding it up!"

Out on the sidewalk, Jeff looked at his watch. It was almost one o'clock. "I don't know about you guys," he said, "but I'm getting hungry."

Everyone nodded in unison.

Kenan looked at the team. "I've got two more hours. Then I'll need to head back to pick up Parmelee and Warren."

"I think we should go with you," Mindy worried.

K.J. rolled his eyes. "Hey, we'll be okay. We've taken the bus trip a couple of times now. Besides, Warren wants us to get footage of the palace."

Mindy grimaced. "We'd better not get in any more trouble, K.J., or I'll hang you upside down by your video cables." Jeff shot Mindy a warning glance, and she remembered that she had caused some trouble too. She had lost the diary.

Kenan shaded his eyes from the glaring sun. "I'll write out directions to the palace for you in Turkish. Just show the driver, and he'll take you there."

"What if we meet up with the Brotherhood?" Mindy wondered, unconvinced.

Kenan shrugged. "Look. If you guys want to go home after lunch, it's okay with me. But you might as well work on the video."

Jeff nodded. "Kenan's right, Mindy. Besides, we'll be in crowds all day. We'll be safe."

K.J. was getting impatient. "Would you guys hurry up and resolve this? I'm starved."

Kenan agreed. "I'd like to take you to a Turkish restaurant, unless you'd rather go to Pizza Hut."

"No way!" K.J. said. "We can have that at home. My mom sometimes barbecues meat on little skewers. She said they were Turkish. Got any of those?"

"Um. Sounds good to me," Mindy smiled.

"Let's go, then," Kenan ordered. "I know just the place."

The words on the front of the restaurant said "The Pembe Kosk." Standing on Marmara Shore Road, Kenan explained that the Sea of Marmara was only a few hundred yards below.

"We must be close to the Blue Mosque, then," Jeff said. "We'll need to get some footage of it, too."

"First, I need food," K.J. growled like a hungry animal. "We hardly ate anything yesterday. I intend to make up for lost time."

Everyone agreed, laughing together.

Jeff was awed when they walked in the restaurant. The ancient building was richly decorated with expensive lamps, carpets and decorations. Paintings showing Turkish culture hung on the stone walls, and the air smelled as much like cigarette smoke as it did food.

After being seated, a waiter handed them menus, which Jeff hid behind while he scanned the restaurant for bearded men. He finally relaxed and looked at what the menu said, surprised to see the words written in English. They must cater to tourists, he thought.

K.J. waved his hand in front of his face to disperse the cigarette smoke that hung in clouds around them.

"Why do so many people smoke here?" he asked. "Don't they know it causes cancer?"

"Some say it's the way we keep warm in the winter," Kenan said. "I'm sure it's just a bad habit."

Jeff put down his menu. "What do you recommend for lunch?"

"What K.J. wanted was shish kebab—meat on a skewer with tomatoes and onions, grilled on a charcoal fire. Chicken and lamb are popular, but they serve beef and fish, too."

"Most of that sounds good to me," K.J. moaned. "But I don't like the idea of eating a fuzzy little lamb."

Mindy giggled, then turned to Kenan. "How about ordering one of each, except the lamb. Then we can try them all."

They all nodded.

K.J. smacked his lips. "What else?"

"We can also get a salad and some vegetables."

K.J. grinned from ear to ear. "I think I'm liking Istanbul more and more."

"What shall we get to drink?" Mindy asked.

"If you order cola, they'll bring you either Coke or Pepsi, whichever they have," Kenan said. "Or you could try Iran—it's like a salty, watery yogurt."

"No thanks," Jeff said, wrinkling his nose. "Let's stick to the cola."

Kenan chuckled. "Turkish meals also end with coffee or strong Turkish tea. Will you want some?"

All together, they shook their heads.

With that decided, Kenan ordered for them, and soon after, the table was filled with delicious platters of food. Jeff took a deep breath. He couldn't believe the wonderful aroma rising from the sizzling meat. He ate feeling like a king.

"Kenan," he said, laying an empty skewer across his gold-rimmed plate, "I remember reading about Turkish delight in C.S. Lewis' books. Could we try some?"

Kenan finished his last bite and checked his watch. "Sure, but it's getting late. Let's order some quickly."

K.J.'s eyes lit up. "I remember reading about that too. What is Turkish delight?"

"Candy. Kind of like jelly beans but without the

outer covering. It's good. Sweets are a big thing around here."

When he had gotten the waiter's attention and everyone had tried the sweet treat, Kenan pulled out some Turkish liras to pay the bill. Then he looked at his watch again.

"It's 2:30. I'll take you on the bus to the palace, since there's time. Then I'll have to leave."

"I just hope we're doing the right thing," Mindy said nervously.

Chapter 7

Lost

Jeff couldn't believe his eyes as he gazed up at Topkapi Sarayi Palace. Built on one of Istanbul's seven hills, it was located on land that jutted out between the Bosphorus and the Golden Horn. Jeff was lost in its beauty.

Mindy broke into his thoughts.

"Since Kenan isn't here, I'll be your tour guide. I studied this place. Right this way," she said, bowing dramatically.

K.J. quickly got his camera rolling.

"This is where the sultans—the rulers of Turkish

empires—used to live," Mindy explained. "It's like our White House. They controlled the Turkish Empire, which was called the Ottoman Empire in those days."

Jeff stared up at the architecture. "This is amazing."

"It sure is," Mindy smiled. "For four centuries, this was the home of some of Turkey's greatest rulers. It's the most fascinating work of Turkish architecture."

Jeff gazed at the highest tower. "When was it built?"

"Mehmet the Conqueror built it shortly after the Turks took over in 1453. It was used until the mid 1800s, when the new sultan decided he wanted a European-style palace."

K.J. took the camera down from his face. "How do you remember all this stuff? No wonder you always ace your history classes."

"Research is my job," Mindy said, tapping a pencil on her notes.

K.J. just shook his head.

As the team toured different sections of the palace, Jeff studied a map of the building. There were four courts. The First court was open to the public and contained a hospital, a bakery, an arsenal, the state mint, and storage. The Second served as the administration center, and the Third was reserved for government officials and members of the Sultan's household.

But the Fourth court was the crowded one. Surrounded by colorful gardens and pools, it was where the sultan lived.

As they walked along, they were amazed at the things kept under security glass. There was priceless jewelry, ornate swords—even beard hairs from Mohammed.

K.J. got it all on tape.

It was six o'clock when Jeff realized it was time to go.

"We should leave," he said. "I can't wait to meet Kenan's wife. And to see Warren."

"If we ever get home," Mindy moaned as they walked out. "I hope Kenan wrote good directions."

K.J. struggled to keep his camera bag over his shoulder. "I got some amazing shots of this place. I can't wait to edit this stuff. It's gonna be some of my best work."

Jeff nodded in agreement.

Anxious to get home, the team headed for the bus stop where they had gotten off.

Jeff looked at the paper with the directions. "Okay. We wait for the number ten bus. Then we'll show the driver our directions and be on our way."

Mindy sat down and tried to smile. It seemed the team waited forever. Jeff remembered what Kenan said about buses taking time. Even with your own car, Jeff suspected the traffic jams were still terrible.

His watch said it was seven. Suddenly, he grew cold. He stared into the crowd. Then focusing his eyes, he gasped.

It was Abdullah. With four bearded men.

Jeff didn't want to tell Mindy, but it was too late. Mindy gasped in fright.

"Look. It's those guys!" she screamed. "They're heading right for us."

"What do we do?" K.J. cried.

Jeff looked around and spotted a bus loading across the street. He had to make a quick decision. "Quick. Let's catch that one. It's ready to leave."

"What number is it?" Mindy asked, gathering her bag.

"Who cares?" Jeff reasoned, pulling her across the street by the hand. "Let's get out of here."

"Wait. It's number four," Mindy protested. "The wrong one."

"It doesn't matter. Let's go," he demanded.

They were the last people to get on. The other passengers eyed them curiously. They had boarded in such a hurry.

Jeff couldn't stand not looking. He saw the men crossing the street. As he shot a prayer toward heaven, the men ran for the bus. Closer and closer. He didn't want to think about what would happen if they got on board.

Mindy almost exploded with anxiety. As a scream formed in her throat, the driver shut the door. Through the glass, Jeff saw Abdullah standing in front of the door, staring into the bus.

"Look," Mindy said lowly. "There's a kid with a scar standing with Abdullah. He must be the one who took my diary!"

"You're right, Mindy. It must be him." Jeff held his breath, praying hard.

Thankfully, the driver was looking in the rear view mirror rather than at the door. He pulled into traffic just as Abdullah raised his fist to beat on the glass. The street kid look frightened. Abdullah shook his fist in anger. Jeff knew the team would run into them again.

Tears filled Mindy's eyes. "They must have my diary. That kid is with them."

"It looks that way," Jeff said quietly, slouching down in his seat. "We've had it now."

"I'm not going anywhere alone in this city again," Mindy vowed. "If Kenan or Warren doesn't go, I'm not either."

"I'm sorry, sis," Jeff sighed. "I don't want to go alone anymore either. But remember, if we hadn't gotten in that accident, Warren would have been with us."

"Maybe he couldn't have done anything either," Mindy lamented, looking at Jeff and K.J. for an answer.

Neither of them knew what to say.

When the bus crossed the familiar Galata Bridge, they all felt better.

"I think this bus is taking us to the right place," K.J. said.

"It probably runs the same route," Jeff agreed. "Besides I have Kenan's directions in my pocket."

As Jeff reached into his pocket to get them, a young boy walked up to the man in front of him and poured lemon cologne over his hands. Then he went down the aisle doing the same thing to the others.

Jeff remembered Kenan saying that this was for the passengers to refresh themselves. Everyone thanked the boy, then splashed the cologne on their faces.

"This is a good idea," K.J. smiled, combing some into his hair. "I think they should do this in America."

Again, Jeff reached for the directions. An empty feeling crept into his stomach as he felt around the bottom of his pocket. The paper was gone. Frantically searching his other pockets, he couldn't hide his panic.

Mindy noticed instantly. "What is it, Jeff?"

Still patting his pockets, Jeff hesitated. As they

bounced along, he looked under the seat. The bus stopped, letting off passengers.

"Maybe we should get off," K.J. said, his voice trembling.

Jeff wished Warren was there. Again, he had to make a decision. The bus was getting ready to go again.

Sheepishly, Jeff looked at K.J. and Mindy. "I'm sorry. I seem to have lost the directions. But I know we'll get home. Let's stay on this bus until it takes us over the Bosphorus."

Mindy held back tears. "It's getting dark. We could get lost."

"We'll be okay, Mindy," Jeff said weakly. "We'll be okay."

The sound of the bus engines roared, settling Jeff's decision.

Darkness fell quickly over Istanbul. The bus bumped along. Jeff and the club kept their eyes glued on the road ahead.

"Look. We're heading for the Bosphorus Bridge now," Jeff pointed excitedly. "I knew this bus was heading the right direction."

K.J. and Mindy drew deep breaths in relief.

"Even if it weren't the right bus," K.J. laughed, "anything is better than being with Abdullah and his friends."

Mindy's eyes were troubled. "Well, I agree with that. But they may find us again."

K.J. looked surprised. "Do you think they just happened to be there? Or were they following us?"

"I don't know," Jeff said, shrugging his shoulders. "I hope it was just a coincidence."

Bumper to bumper traffic delayed their trip over the bridge. Finally, the bus finished its slow crawl to the other side.

"Do you think this will get us close to Kenan's?" asked K.J.

"I hope so," Jeff said. "It's hard to tell in the dark. But I've got Kenan's phone number if we get lost. I'll just have to figure out how to speak Turkish."

"Oh great," K.J. muttered. "Really great."

As the bus bounced along, everyone stared out the window, hoping. The moments passed quickly.

"Shouldn't we ask the driver?" Mindy reasoned.

Jeff shook his head. "He probably doesn't speak English. Let's wait a while longer. Maybe we'll recognize Kenan's neighborhood."

Time passed. When Jeff didn't see any familiar landmarks, he knew something was wrong. Out the window, he saw a large body of water. Mindy saw it at the same time.

"Look. We're really lost, aren't we?" she demanded. "We've been on this thing for over an hour."

Jeff didn't know what to say. He felt helpless.

K.J. stared out the window in disbelief. "We are lost!"

Chapter 8

Murat

Jeff knew they were right. He had to do something. But he didn't even know the Turkish word for stop. They were getting further and further from the mission house. As the bus rolled along, he realized they hadn't been in a situation quite like this before. He didn't know what to do.

The other passengers seemed to be settling down to sleep, and Jeff realized they were heading across country. A slow tension started to build inside. He couldn't even look K.J. or Mindy's way.

Jeff gritted his teeth. He glanced at his watch. Eight

o'clock. He knew he couldn't wait any longer. He had to act.

Jeff unfolded himself from his seat and made his way up to the driver. He mumbled a few words, but the driver only looked confused. The man didn't understand a word.

After a moment, the driver pulled to the side of the road and turned on a light. Jeff nervously ran his fingers through his blonde hair. His face turned red as passengers stared. They looked concerned for the team so obviously out of place.

Jeff remembered what Kenan had said about the Turkish people. He hoped they'd be as hospitable as Kenan said they'd be.

Deciding he had nothing to lose, Jeff addressed the passengers in slow, clear English. He hoped someone would understand.

One glance told him that K.J. and Mindy wanted to disappear from the face of the earth. So did he. But since he was the leader, he had to take charge. Warren had trained him to handle tough situations.

Jeff listened as the driver spoke to the passengers. Finally, a man got up and came forward.

"We're lost," Jeff said slowly, trying to make him understand.

"Where do you live?" the man asked with a heavy Turkish accent.

Jeff felt foolish. Because he'd lost the paper, he didn't know how to answer. Then he remembered how close the mission house was to the Bosphorus Bridge.

"Near the big bridge," Jeff said. "The big bridge."

The man chuckled to himself. Pulling out a small map, he pointed to a body of water. Jeff was stunned.

They were far north of the mission house, near Beykoz. The body of water was the Black Sea.

"I'll help," the man assured him.

Jeff felt relief. "Thank you, sir," he said, offering his hand. "I'm very grateful."

Jeff waited as the man explained to the driver, then to the passengers, what had happened. Jeff was grateful that no one laughed. As the bus started up again, Jeff panicked a little.

But the man smiled. "Another bus. You go back to big bridge. Phone home," he said, taking a seat near the team.

Jeff was relieved. The man seemed to understand where they needed to go.

Ten minutes passed. Jeff knew Warren and Kenan would be worried sick by now, but there was nothing he could do.

He turned to the man again. "Would you mind making a call for us to get directions?" The man didn't understand.

Mindy moved closer. "Let me try, Jeff."

She made a gesture of being on the phone. "Phone call," she said, pointing to the man. "We need you to help us make the call."

Just then the bus pulled over, and the man led them off. As the bus pulled away, the passengers smiled warmly and waved. The team waved back.

Jeff looked around. He realized they were in front of some kind of restaurant. He scanned the street for a phone, but his eyes were drawn to the bus, stopping again further down the road. The passengers were still smiling and waving at them. At that instant, just before the bus disappeared into the darkness, Jeff felt a special love for the Turkish people.

The team followed the man inside the restaurant. To everyone's relief, they spotted a pay phone. The man pulled change from his pocket. Jeff waited. The man looked at him. "Number. You have number?"

Reaching into his back pocket, Jeff pulled out his wallet, and handed the man the card where he'd written Kenan's number.

As the man dialed, everyone held their breath. Jeff prayed it was the right number. After talking to the operator, the man nodded and smiled.

Jeff smiled too as they waited. Then his face fell. He knew by the man's face that there was no answer.

"No one home," the man said, shrugging his shoulders.

"Where could they be?" Jeff wondered.

"Probably at the police station looking for us," K.J. mumbled.

"You're probably right," Mindy said, gnawing at her lower lip. "And with Warren's broken leg, he couldn't get to the phone anyway."

"What do we do now?" Jeff asked.

The man looked into Jeff's eyes kindly and pointed. "New bus. Back to bridge. Then call."

Jeff nodded in agreement and shook the man's hand. They didn't try to talk much while they waited.

After a half hour, another bus arrived. This one appeared to be going in the right direction. But then Jeff had thought that before.

The team followed their new friend to the parked bus. He talked to the driver while Jeff waited.

"New bus," he said when he was finished. "Bosphorus Bridge."

Jeff felt like giving the man a giant hug goodbye, but he settled on a big handshake. Mindy and K.J. did the same.

The tired club climbed on board. Barely able to keep his eyes open, Jeff started to question God about why He let them get lost. After a moment, he realized it was partly his fault for losing the paper.

Bouncing along, he wrestled with his thoughts. Jeff wanted to blame somebody for all their problems. He felt like punching Abdullah, but he knew that there was a deeper reason for everything that had happened that day.

On all their trips, God had shown the club over and over how He could use tough circumstances for His good. They would have to trust Him one more time.

Too tired to think any more, Jeff laid his head against the back of the seat.

Mindy and K.J. sat across the aisle. Rolling his head lazily to the side, he looked at the person next to him. Reflected in the window were a sad pair of dark eyes and a full head of dark, curly hair.

The man was Turkish, about the same build as Warren, and looked to be around thirty or thirty-five. He was staring out the window, and appeared to be deep in thought. Jeff decided not to bother him and laid his head back down.

Just then, the stranger spoke to him in perfect English. Jeff looked up, surprised.

The stranger glanced over at Jeff. "The man said you're in some kind of trouble."

"Not trouble exactly. We're lost."

Maybe it was his unshaved face, but Jeff thought the man looked depressed.

The stranger sat up straight, offering his hand. "My name is Murat."

Jeff introduced himself. He spent the next few minutes explaining what had happened. Then he introduced Mindy and K.J., and together they told him about the club. They were thrilled to be talking to a Turk in English.

"Do you believe in God?" Murat asked.

"Yes," Jeff replied, surprised again. "That's why we came here."

Murat turned to stare out the window. When he turned back, he looked Jeff straight in the eye. "I know why you got lost," he said, his eyes moist with tears.

Jeff waited. By now, K.J. and Mindy were leaning way over to listen.

"You got lost so you could help me."

Chapter 9

The Collapse

Jeff was astonished. "What do you mean?" he asked.

"I've had no one I could talk to. For some reason it's easy to talk to you."

Jeff turned to face him in the seat. Mindy and K.J. were leaning in so close that they filled the whole aisle.

Murat took a deep breath. "I'm not a Christian. I'm a Muslim." He barely moved his lips. "I'm very depressed."

Jeff waited. And prayed.

"I'm on the way home from my brother's house."

He let out a sigh that sounded as if he'd been carrying an enormous burden. "You see, my wife left me a few days ago. She took my two children and all the money with her. I was so angry I didn't know what I would do to her."

Mindy's eyes grew bigger than ever, but she didn't say a word. K.J. was silent too. Jeff knew they were praying.

Jeff rubbed his tired eyes in confusion. "But what's that got to do with us getting lost?"

Murat held his head in his hands for a moment. Jeff saw his pain and was anxious to help, but he honestly didn't know how. Perhaps Murat just needed someone to listen. And to care.

Finally, Murat looked up again. "I planned to go home this afternoon to get even with my wife—hurt her because she hurt me...I don't know. But then my brother's little girl got sick, and I couldn't get to the bus. I was delayed over and over. I missed three buses before I got on this one."

Smiling to himself, Jeff realized they weren't lost. They were in God's perfect will.

Murat continued. "I was so angry. I know I would have really hurt her. The only thing stopping me was my children." Murat paused to wipe his tears with his sleeve. "I love my kids so much. But my wife and I have had too many problems. I don't know what to do."

Jeff blinked hard, fighting back the tears that threatened to fall in his lap. He knew God was at work. Sadness filled his heart thinking how much he'd questioned God about letting them get lost.

Jeff looked at Murat. "How do you know your wife took the money?"

Murat's eyelids shot up like a rocket. "I know she did. She took the kids and left me alone for two days. So I decided to go to my brother's house. I was furious and so was my brother. He told me to go home and let her have it."

Jeff listened carefully. His heart broke for this man he'd just met.

Murat went on. "All day I heard this voice inside me, warning me not to hurt my wife. But I was really angry."

Murat wept. Other passengers looked at them. Jeff didn't care. God was at work.

After a few moments, Murat looked up and removed his hands from his eyes. "Sunday is my daughter's tenth birthday. I want her to have a happy day, but I'm afraid I'll ruin it with my anger."

Jeff remained silent. He knew Murat needed time to think. And it sounded to him like God was speaking to Murat's heart.

Jeff's words almost surprised him when he spoke again. "I'd like to pray with you."

First, he saw anger flare up in Murat's eyes. Murat stiffened and backed up a few inches.

"I'm sorry," Jeff said quickly. "I just want to help you."

Murat began to spit out angry words. "I'm tired of praying. As a Muslim, I've prayed five times a day, every day of my life. I've even been to Mecca. It's supposed to make you holier. But I don't feel holy. Things are worse. I think religion stinks."

Now Jeff understood. "I'm sorry for offending you by asking you to pray. But I don't think it's an accident we've met. Even you said that God put us together for a reason."

Murat didn't say anything.

"Maybe you can help us find our way home," Jeff said. "And we'll pray that your problems will work out."

Murat softened and he nodded. "The man said you need to get off near the Bosphorus Bridge. I'll help you call your friends."

Jeff reached out to shake Murat's hand, and Murat accepted.

Sitting quietly the rest of the trip, Jeff realized he had to be careful not to offend Murat. But Jeff knew the power of prayer. Murat was sick of rules and religion. What he needed was a relationship with God. Jeff knew God would have to show him.

The Bosphorus Bridge was a welcome sight for everyone. Anxiously, they climbed off the bus and found a telephone. Murat dialed the numbers.

Everyone waited. When Murat smiled and began to speak to someone in Turkish, Jeff and the others almost leaped for joy. After a minute, Murat handed Jeff the phone.

Jeff took it excitedly. "Hello," he cried. "Hello."

Jeff listened. It was Kenan's voice. After a few words of explanation, he handed Murat the phone again to get directions. Finally, Murat hung up.

"There," Murat said. "I'll take you home. Until I figure out what I'm going to do, I can't go home anyway."

Murat stepped to the street and hailed a taxi. Moments later, they were speeding toward Kenan's house. Mindy and K.J. looked as exhausted as Jeff felt. Jeff was amazed at how gracious Murat was to stay with them.

Finally, the taxi screeched to a stop in front of Kenan's house.

"Boy, is that a wonderful sight!" Mindy said happily.

"Yeah," K.J. echoed. "Home sweet home."

Murat's eyes flared suddenly again. "I probably won't have a home in a few hours," he groaned.

Realizing what he had said, K.J. apologized.

Jeff reached for Murat's hand and smiled. "I can't thank you enough, Murat. I know you'll do the right thing. And if you want to talk again, come back any time. I'm not going anywhere for a while."

Murat smiled at each of them before the taxi sped away. The team waved goodbye, then hurried into the house.

Jeff turned to the others on the way up the stone steps. "We need to keep praying for him."

Seeing Kenan sitting next to Warren brought new life to the weary club. The team took turns spilling out the details of what had happened—seeing the Brotherhood and the boy who might have stolen the diary, the bus trip, and meeting Murat.

Jeff stopped when a young woman gracefully entered the room. She wore an elegant skirt and blouse, richly printed in blues and purples. Long, dark hair that looked as soft as silk was piled on her head in loose curls.

Kenan stood up. He took her hand and, with his

voice full of pride, introduced her. "This is Parmelee, my wonderful wife."

Jeff shook her hand, and she greeted the others warmly. When she smiled, her dark eyes seemed to dance.

"It's nice to meet you," Parmelee said. "I'm very sorry for your troubles. Welcome to our home."

Mindy's smile broadened. "We're okay now. Kenan told us a little about how you got together. He said you would tell us the rest."

Parmelee's smile dazzled them all. Jeff knew it was more than physical beauty he observed. Her eyes radiated the love of Jesus.

"I'd be glad to tell you our story," she assured them. "But you must be very tired tonight. How about tomorrow at breakfast?"

Mindy didn't argue. Jeff could see she looked exhausted.

He moved over to sit near Warren. "So, how are you doing?"

Warren grimaced in pain as he tried to pull himself up. "Not too bad. I've got my new cast," he said, showing it off.

"Can we sign it?" K.J. asked with a gleam in his eye.

Warren tried to laugh. "Sure. But let's save that for morning too." His face turned serious. "I'm proud of you guys. We were worried about you. But we prayed, and God took good care of you."

Kenan smiled. "God is good to bring my friends safely home," he said, looking at his tired guests. "Why don't we go to bed? Tomorrow I'm going to show you our literature depot. It's an old building where we store the literature visiting teams hand out when they're here."

Jeff and K.J. cast big smiles at Kenan.

"Any news on my diary?" Mindy had to ask.

Warren shook his head.

Jeff looked at their host. "Can we do one other thing before we go to bed?"

"What's that?" Kenan asked.

"Can we pray for Murat? I know God is working in him."

Warren and Kenan nodded, and they all joined hands, kneeling around Warren so he could join them.

Jeff looked up to heaven. "Lord, please show Murat You are the true God. Show him that Jesus is the Answer he seeks. Give him wisdom to do the right thing with his wife. Amen."

Saturday morning, the sun rose brightly, scattering the night and taking possession of the day. Jeff was still tired after all that had happened the day before. Lying with his hands behind his head, he couldn't get Murat off his mind. He knew prayer was the key to the situation.

As the breakfast bell rang, the hungry team headed to the dining room. Parmelee and Kenan placed plates on the table. Besides the eggs and rolls the team might have eaten at home, they also served traditional Turkish breakfast foods. There were olives, tomatoes, cheese and yogurt on the side.

Warren looked longingly toward the table from his spot on the couch. Jeff took him a plate of food, then sat with the others. The team prayed and dug into the delicious breakfast.

"Parmelee," Mindy said between bites, "I'd still like to hear how you two fell in love. Do we have time?"

Wiping her mouth with a napkin, Parmelee smiled. "After Kenan became a Christian, the Lord gave me a dream. He showed me I would marry him."

Mindy's mouth fell open. "That's neat!"

"God had to show us that clearly," Parmelee explained. "We knew our families would have trouble with an Armenian marrying a Turk. But by our wedding day, both families gave us their blessing."

"Parmelee," Jeff wondered, "your family has always been Christian. How did Kenan's parents handle your beliefs?"

Parmelee smiled at the memory. "We prayed for his family every day while we were engaged. Of course, they were opposed at first. In Turkey, engagement almost means the same thing as marriage. In a few months, Kenan's mom became a Christian, then introduced his dad to the Lord."

"That's a miracle!" K.J. exclaimed. "Did his parents suffer persecution?"

"Yes. A number of their friends rejected them," Parmelee said. "But God has given them some new ones."

Mindy was beaming. Everyone smiled. They knew how much she loved a happy ending.

"Kenan," Jeff said after a few minutes, "you said you would finish telling us about Istanbul. How about now?"

Kenan nodded. "Actually, the stories weave together."

Kenan sipped his strong, Turkish coffee, and Jeff sat back to listen.

"Here's a little history of Istanbul," Kenan began. "When Paul preached here, it was to the Greeks in Byzantium. But Constantine conquered Byzantium in 324 A.D. and made it the capitol in 330. He wanted it to be the greatest city in the world—the new Rome. His dream finally came true."

"How's that?" K.J. asked.

"He started a building program in the city. It has never been equaled for speed and extravagance. Laborers came from all over the world, even from Rome."

Everyone leaned in, especially Mindy.

"Constantine was the first Christian Roman emperor," Kenan continued, "the new head of church and state. The story goes he once had a vision in the noonday sky. He saw a fiery cross with the words written in flames: 'By this sign, conquer.'"

They all listened in amazement.

"This was the sign, as the story goes, by which he was converted to Christianity."

"Didn't he make Christianity the official religion?" Mindy asked.

"Yes," Kenan nodded. "No one is quite sure whether it was a political move or the real thing. But I know this. It messed everything up by making Christianity the popular thing to do. It stopped being a change of heart and became a change of values. Kind of a moral conversion."

"Wow," Warren exclaimed from his place on the couch. "There's a lesson to learn."

Kenan nodded seriously. "It led to the ultimate

downfall. As centuries passed, Mohammed appeared, seeing the phony things that sometimes come with religion—like dead faith and coldness. As his movement grew, a roaming band of warriors called the Turks met up with his followers. Having no religion, they completely converted to Islam."

"I can't believe I haven't heard this before," Jeff said. "What happened next?"

"Well," Kenan replied, "they immediately began attacking Christian strongholds, and around 1100 they set out to conquer the world. This sparked the organized attacks against Islam known as the Crusades. That's why Muslims accuse Christianity of using guns instead of love."

"That's why I've heard so many bad things about the Crusades," Jeff said. "How could that happen?"

"Easily," Kenan explained. "As the Turks became aggressive, the church in Rome started sending armies to fight them. It wasn't long until the purpose of defending Christianity during the First Crusade got lost. The men got greedy for what they could get."

"What do you mean?" K.J. asked.

"Well, by the time the fifteen hundred appointed knights and infantry were ready to advance, a wild group of three thousand joined, charging across Europe. They pillaged, vandalized, and indulged in every evil in the name of Christ. It got real ugly. The later Crusades were the same."

"I've been reading about this," Mindy said, "and it always makes me feel terrible."

"It's sad," Kenan agreed. "The crusaders became so rotten that they robbed Jerusalem. Enraged by rumors that the Jews of Palestine had instigated the Muslim attacks, the crusaders massacred unarmed Jews in every city, town and village."

"Wow," Jeff gasped.

"Then they attacked Constantinople on the way down. The Crusades so weakened the city that the Ottoman Empire finally broke through the walled fortress at noon on May 29, 1453. That marked the end of Christianity in this part of the world."

Parmelee spoke softly. "Now you can understand the hatred for Christianity in this part of the world. But we feel God wants to break through all the hatred. Our marriage is a testimony to that."

"That's beautiful," Mindy said. "But I can see why these Brotherhood guys are so mad. The hate has been around for centuries."

While Jeff thought about what he had heard, Kenan got up to answer the phone. Moments later, he rushed back in.

"What's wrong?" Parmelee cried out.

"It's our storage depot."

"What is it?" she pressed.

"A wall collapsed."

Chapter 10

Busted

Jeff couldn't believe it.

"How did that happen?" Warren asked.

"It's a very old building. The inside wall fell and left holes on the outside. A friend who lives nearby called to tell me he saw kids trying to steal some stuff."

"Did they get anything?" Jeff asked.

"Not yet," Kenan replied. "There's nothing inside but some Gospel of John books and Christian correspondence courses. I guess the kids left a bunch of them laying in the street."

"Uh oh," Jeff lamented. "That could be trouble. Can we help?"

Kenan looked at Parmelee, who shrugged her shoulders and waited for him to reply.

"Maybe one or two can," Kenan said. "But we need to hurry. If the police find that stuff, we'll all be in trouble."

Mindy walked over to Parmelee. "I'll stay with Parmelee and help with the dishes."

Jeff knew Mindy had had her quota of trouble. He was glad she was going to stay with Warren and Parmelee.

Jeff, K.J. and Kenan headed to the depot in a taxi. Kenan hoped to get there before the wrong people found the literature.

Jeff turned to Kenan, who looked deep in thought. "How much stuff did you have there?"

"There were about forty thousand Gospels of John and two thousand correspondence courses. People who have questions about the Bible begin to learn with these correspondence studies."

K.J. was surprised. "Why so many?"

"We had planned to give out sixty thousand last summer, but the police started cracking down. Our visiting teams were only able to give out twenty thousand, so we stored what was left."

"What if the police found them?" Jeff asked.

Before Kenan answered, the taxi pulled over to the curb. Jeff and K.J. didn't see anything.

"The storage building is a block away," Kenan explained. "To be safe, I'd like to walk the rest of the way."

They were in an area of run-down, collapsing buildings. As they made their way down the street, Kenan slowed to a stop. Cautiously, he proceeded. Jeff followed. K.J. flattened himself against the brick wall as if he were a character in a spy novel.

Suddenly, Kenan stepped back from the corner of the old building. His eyes were wide with alarm.

"They've got it," he said.

"What happened, Kenan?" Jeff begged. "What is it?"

"Careful. Take a look," Kenan said.

Slowly, Jeff peeked around the corner. He couldn't believe it. Three policemen stood there. His heart sank. Behind them, Abdullah and the Brotherhood were busy stuffing the literature into trash bags.

Jeff turned back. "Now what?"

"The stuff is lost now," Kenan said, shaking his head. "We'll never be able to use that building again. But for now, we need to get out of here. If Abdullah spots us...I don't want to think about it."

Jeff and K.J. tiptoed behind Kenan. As soon as they were safe, Kenan called a taxi.

Once inside, no one said a word. Jeff felt like the walls were falling in on all of them. He could only pray and watch the Istanbul neighborhoods rush by.

Even K.J. knew it was a time to be silent.

Back at the house, Jeff and K.J. explained to Warren and Mindy what had happened. Kenan and Parmelee had gone up to their room to talk.

"Why is all this happening?" Jeff asked. "Can't any-body stop Abdullah from his attacks? Doesn't the man have anything else to do? No family? No job?"

Warren struggled to sit up. "Jeff, God is at work. And the enemy too. Kenan will know what to do."

Soon, Kenan and Parmelee came down from their room holding hands. They sat down with the team.

"I'm sorry for the difficulties," Kenan apologized.

"You're sorry?" K.J. said. "We didn't help your cause."

"This has happened before," Kenan said with a sad smile.

"Will the police come after you?" Mindy asked.

"I don't think so. The building is registered in the name of a man who died a year ago."

"Does Abdullah know it's your depot?" Jeff asked.

"I hope not," Kenan replied. "He knows a lot about Christian activity. After all, he was one of us. We'll get a visit soon if he does."

"What about the neighbor?" K.J. asked.

"He's a believer. He was just keeping an eye on the place for me."

"Can you get more literature?" Mindy asked.

"Yes, although I hate to waste what we had. Several organizations donate it. The police have busted buildings before, so we just keep moving it around."

Suddenly, Mindy got excited. "Hey, I just remembered. I have some good news. While you were out, I found the names of those Turkish believers! They were in one of my computer files. I've even got the name of their church."

"That's great, Mindy," Kenan said. "I'll call the pastor to let him know what happened. He can warn the families to be on the lookout."

K.J. leaned forward. "You know, I'll never complain about how hard it is to be a Christian in an American high school again. I think I know what tough is now."

Suddenly, everyone jumped at the sound of a loud knock on the front door.

Chapter 11

Revelation

"What if it's Abdullah?"

"Or the police?" K.J. cried.

Everyone was on their feet. Kenan squeezed Parmelee's hand, then went to the door. Just as he reached to open it, someone knocked again, practically rattling it out of his hand.

Everyone stood still. Mindy moved closer to Jeff. He heard a familiar voice, but he couldn't think of whose it was.

Kenan hurried back, looking relieved. "There's someone here to see you, Jeff."

Jeff rushed to the door. When he rounded the corner, his eyes nearly popped out of his head. It was Murat!

Jeff almost jumped with excitement. "Come in, Murat," he invited. "Please meet my friends."

While introducing him, Jeff noticed something different. As they sat down, Murat smiled at everyone, a smile that seemed to come from somewhere deep in his soul. The anger and depression were gone.

K.J. slipped out to grab his camera.

"It's nice to meet you," Murat said graciously. "I'm so excited to be here. I'm sure Jeff told you how angry I was last night. But things are different now."

"What happened?" Jeff asked excitedly.

Murat spoke quietly. "Last night, I was on my way to attack my wife—I really wanted to hurt her. But when I got home, I couldn't get angry."

Jeff smiled. He knew what had happened.

"I asked my wife if we could talk things out in the morning. Then I hurried off to the guest room."

Everyone leaned forward.

"Well, after I fell asleep, I had a most unusual dream. A man appeared to me in a dream—standing at the foot of my bed. In a flood of light, he told me that He is the true Messiah and the Son of the living God!"

Everyone listened in awe. With tears in his eyes, Murat went on.

"The man said His name was Jesus. He told me to worship Him."

Tears ran down Jeff's face. He could see tears falling behind the lens of K.J.'s camera. With a huge smile on her face, Mindy was crying too.

"Immediately, I fell to my knees, worshiping at his

feet," Murat recounted. "It was amazing. The room was filled with the warmest light I've ever known."

Jeff kept shaking his head in wonder. God had answered their prayer.

Murat started to sob. "I have become a believer in Jesus."

Kenan got up. Hurrying over, he gave Murat a hug and spoke to him in Turkish. Jeff watched Kenan's love for his people. Though his host had experienced a hard day, Jeff saw love in action.

Murat wiped his eyes, smiling through his tears.

"What about your wife, Murat?" Jeff asked.

"Things are different now. When I woke up, I told her how much I loved her and admitted where I've been wrong. Then I forgave her for what she did. She couldn't believe it."

"That's great!" Jeff cried joyfully.

"Not only that," Murat said, "but she knew something was different about me. I told her about meeting you on the bus ride and about the dream."

"What did she say?" Warren asked.

"Well, that's why I'm here. I have three requests."

Jeff leaned forward.

"First," Murat said, "I need to know what to do next. Second, my wife wants to find out more about Christianity. Would you help me explain it to her? I don't quite understand it myself." Murat wiped his eyes again. "Third, my wife wants to meet all of you. We're having a birthday party for my daughter tomorrow evening. We nearly canceled it because we were fighting, but my wife wants to have it now. I want all of you to come. We can talk to my wife after the guests leave."

Jeff looked at the others, especially Kenan.

Kenan shrugged and smiled. "We have nothing planned. We'd be delighted to come. It will be good for the team to attend a Turkish birthday party. They'll have a lot of fun."

Jeff felt as if he might float away. This was one of the greatest miracles he had seen.

"Jeff," Kenan suggested, "why don't you talk with Murat while I make a call to that pastor. I need to let him know about the diary."

Jeff nodded. He knew Murat had lots of questions, and he was glad when Parmelee stayed to help him answer them.

"Have you ever heard of people having dreams like this?" Murat asked.

Jeff turned to Parmelee, who answered quietly.

"Yes. It is happening quite frequently now. I think it's a result of the worldwide prayer movement for this area—what we call the 10/40 window—I'll explain that another day. I heard of one village where Jesus appeared to everyone. He told them the same thing. The whole village was converted."

Jeff suddenly had an idea. Asking to be excused, he ran to his room and grabbed his Bible. When he returned, he was grinning from ear to ear.

"Murat, I want to give you this as a special gift. It was my Bible, but now it's yours."

Murat's eyes filled with tears again. "I don't know how to thank you. I'll always treasure it. I've never read the Bible. I was taught that it's not a good book to read, but now I can't wait to see what it says."

Jeff smiled through his tears. "It's the story of Jesus. Every page will teach you wonderful stories about His life, death, and resurrection. It will teach you to walk in His grace and be free."

Murat began to weep. "I've been looking for freedom all my life. Until now, I've only known fear and bondage."

Jeff smiled at everyone. K.J. put the camera down long enough to share what Jesus meant to him. Jeff was full of gratitude as he listened to Mindy tell Murat about her Lord.

When Kenan returned, his face full of concern.

"What happened?" Jeff asked.

Kenan sighed. "I talked to the pastor. He said strange things have been happening at their church. He believes the Brotherhood must have the diary. Abdullah's been harassing some of his people."

"Oh no," Mindy cried. "That kid must've given it to them."

"Maybe. But I've got some good news too. He's invited you to come to a special service tomorrow morning. They're moving their meeting to a different place. He wants you to share about Murat and the club."

Jeff felt guilt creep into his soul. The team's presence had caused these faithful believers to be in danger.

They had to get the diary back.

Chapter 12

Secret Meeting

Jeff tried to shake his discomfort. "What kind of things have happened?"

"One of the families has had trouble at work," Kenan said. "The pastor can't be sure it's related to the diary, but it made more sense after I told him."

Jeff turned his gaze to Murat, wondering what his thoughts were.

Mindy stared at the floor. "Are the people mad about the diary?"

"They don't know about it, but the pastor said he'd call them tonight."

"I'm so sorry, Kenan," Mindy said quietly. "My carelessness is getting a lot of people in trouble."

Murat looked puzzled. "Young lady," he said, hurrying to Mindy's side, "I don't know exactly what you're talking about here, but I do know that you and your friends helped me. God has changed my life forever." He looked her right in the eye. "I'm sure my decision to follow Jesus will bring me conflict, too. But I'm ready to face anything with Him beside me."

"You're right," Kenan said to Murat. "It won't be easy. Living out the truth costs something."

Just then, Jeff thought of something. "Murat, maybe you can come along tomorrow morning. Would your wife come with you?"

Smiling, Kenan glanced at Parmelee. Then he looked expectantly at Murat. "What do you think?"

"I'd love it. I've never been to a Christian meeting."

Jeff was thrilled at the idea. "Murat could tell his own story. It would be an encouragement to the fellowship."

"That's okay with me," Murat said. "I want to tell everyone I know. But I don't know if my wife will come."

"It's okay if she doesn't," Kenan said, reaching for some paper. He wrote out directions for Murat. "We'll meet at 9:45. The meeting is at ten."

Murat nodded and stood to slip the paper in his pocket. "I'll ask my wife to come, and the kids too," he said, looking at his watch. "I must go now. It's getting late."

Sunday morning sunlight streamed into the room. Jeff awoke wondering what it must have been like to live in the days of Apostle Paul.

Paul had journeyed over every part of this territory. Jeff thought of all the Murats Paul had converted. And of all the persecution.

Jeff scrunched a pillow under him and reached for the Bible Kenan had loaned him. He began to read the Book of Matthew, and his eyes fell upon some of Jesus' words: "I have not come to bring peace, but a sword."

Jeff knew Jesus was the Prince of Peace who brings peace to the soul. But he remembered hearing the Gospel referred to as a sword that divides. Jeff thought about what that might mean to Murat. His family probably wouldn't like the fact that he had accepted Christ.

Listening to K.J. snore, Jeff decided to spend a few more minutes in prayer for Murat and his family. He hoped they would come to the meeting.

The bus rolled up to the curb, near the meeting place. A sudden fear came over Jeff as he stepped down onto the sidewalk. He scanned the length of the street, hoping the Brotherhood wasn't in the area. He knew they had to be careful.

Since Mindy was helping K.J. carry his video equipment, Jeff walked with Kenan and Parmelee.

"Where do you normally go to church on Sunday?" he asked.

Kenan smiled at the thought of his believing friends. "We attend an Armenian fellowship. I called them, and they said they'd be praying for our meeting.

They'd love to hear what's been happening. Maybe you can go with us next Sunday. That will be your last day here, won't it?"

Jeff nodded, then looked at Parmelee. "Are there any Turkish believers in your fellowship?"

"Yes, but it's a rare thing," she said. "Most Greek and Armenian believers don't think Turks can become Christians. That's why I would love for Murat to tell his story to our fellowship, too."

"How many fellowships are there in the city?"

Kenan's smile fell. "Seven or eight. The largest has about forty people."

Just then, Jeff saw Murat waiting in front of the building. Alone.

Jeff rushed over to him. "How are you doing?"

"Okay," Murat said weakly.

By that time, Kenan had caught up. Jeff didn't know what to do. Something was wrong. He hoped silently that Murat would explain.

Murat looked at them through glazed eyes. "My parents and my brother think I'm crazy. They told my wife not to come. Some of the family has decided not to come to my daughter's party tonight."

Jeff remembered the scripture about the sword. He realized that standing for truth can sometimes divide families.

Murat tried to smile, but the pain was too much. "I know what happened to me," he said determinedly. "Nothing can change that. But I wish Jesus would appear to my whole family. It would certainly make things easier."

As Jeff thought about Murat's family, compassion stirred his heart. He offered a silent prayer.

Kenan put his arm around his new brother. "Do you still want to tell your story this morning?"

Murat nodded. But tears welled up in his eyes.

Kenan hugged him. "Let's go," he said turning to the others, who had just joined them. "It's about time for the meeting to begin."

Walking slowly, they followed Kenan up a flight of stairs to a large office building. As they made their way down an inside hall, Jeff thought again of the secret meetings of the early church.

"Do they always meet in secret?" he wondered.

"No, but the pastor is concerned," Kenan explained. "This is a special meeting to talk about the diary. And to hear your team."

Jeff didn't know what to expect. He hoped the lost diary wouldn't create as much of a problem for the pastor as they feared.

Kenan stopped at a doorway. Jeff heard music now. His heart filled with joy when he heard the worship. They were singing from the heart.

Kenan knocked and a middle-aged man opened the door. Jeff assumed he was the pastor.

Kenan turned to the team. "These are my friends from the United States. They're the Reel Kids Adventure Club. And this is Murat—he just became a Christian on Friday!"

The pastor smiled at Murat. When he saw K.J.'s equipment, his face filled with concern. Gently, he put his hand in front of K.J.'s camera. "I know you're a video team, but it just wouldn't be safe for us if our pictures were on tape. I must ask you not to film our faces."

K.J. explained that he would only film from the rear.

"Good," he smiled. "You can speak for about an hour. I'll introduce you to one of the families whose name was written in the diary. The other family may come later."

They followed the pastor to an inner room. Jeff saw a small group of fifteen or twenty people sitting together still singing. Chairs had been saved for the team.

As promised, K.J. and Mindy set up the camera in the rear.

Though the words were sung in Turkish, Jeff recognized the tune of "Amazing Grace." His eyes filled with tears as he began singing along in English. At that moment, Jeff knew what he wanted to share with these people.

After the worship ended, the pastor began to speak. Jeff whispered to Kenan. "What's he saying?"

"He's talking about the diary. And your club."

Jeff listened. Then he heard Kenan's name.

"And about me," Kenan said, getting up.

After some polite applause, Kenan went forward and spoke.

Jeff leaned over to Parmelee. "What's he telling them?"

Parmelee smiled radiantly. "He told them how you got lost." She paused. "And how you've been attacked by the Brotherhood."

When Jeff heard his name, he took a deep breath. Then Kenan nodded to him, and Jeff stood to speak.

"I'm very glad to be here," he said with a friendly smile. "I won't speak long because I want my new friend to tell you what happened to him."

Jeff waited for Kenan's translation.

"I've learned a lot here," Jeff said. "I'm very sad there are so many people in the world who don't know Jesus. Muslims alone make up one-fifth of the earth's population—one billion people."

The people stared with no response.

"God wants us to encourage you this morning. All over the world, there are prayer meetings going on for the Muslim world."

After the translation, Jeff continued.

"God wants to show all people His grace. My friend Murat will tell you that God's grace is amazing, and that when we pray to God in the name of Jesus, God answers." Filled with joy, Jeff shared the freedom he experienced in Christ. Freedom and grace.

Finally he said, "You know, when God looks at the world, He doesn't see one billion Muslims: He sees each person individually, and He loves them. I pray that God will help me love and understand people like He does."

The people were really listening now. Jeff introduced Mindy. She bravely came to the front of the room and apologized for the lost diary.

Finally, Murat stood up. When he told them of the appearance of Jesus in his room, there wasn't a dry eye in the room. The people cheered and warmly welcomed him into God's Kingdom and into their hearts.

Listening to Murat pour out his heart, Jeff realized that God could reach the people in this part of the world.

If only the church would pray, Jeff thought again. At that moment, he realized that this might be God's way for the club to help reach the Muslim people—both the few individuals like Abdullah who had tried to hurt them, and all of the wonderful Turks who had been so kind to their team. Jeff decided to begin challenging Christians around the world to pray for these people that God loved so much, the people Jeff loved now too. He would talk to Mindy and K.J. about making it the theme of the video—calling the church to pray for the 10/40 window.

After the meeting ended, the club stayed for lunch. Jeff noticed how happy and friendly the people were. Kenan had been right about their hospitality.

In the middle of the meal, a tall, thin Turkish man rushed in. His face was tight and strained. He was obviously very upset.

Watching the man approach the pastor, Jeff tried to figure out what was wrong. He hated not knowing what was happening. When he couldn't stand it any longer, he turned to Kenan.

"What's wrong?"

"That man, his name is Engin. He's convinced it's your fault...well, the team's fault...the lost diary's fault, that his hours are being cut at work."

Jeff gulped.

Kenan took a deep breath. "He wants to talk to you."

Chapter 13

Belly Dancing

Jeff felt like running. Not only was the Brotherhood after them, but now a believer was too.

Mindy was so eaten up with guilt that she looked like she might be sick. Jeff walked over and gave her a one-armed hug. "It'll be okay, Mindy. I'll talk to him for you."

Mindy shook her head. "Thanks, big brother, but this is my fault. I shouldn't have been carrying their names around. I need to be there."

Jeff was proud of his sister. She held her head high and marched in beside Jeff and Kenan to meet the angry man. The pastor pointed them to an office where Engin was waiting.

Murat asked if he could attend the meeting, and the man agreed. As soon as the door was closed, Engin began an angry tirade.

Jeff listened uncomfortably.

Kenan looked at his feet, hesitating as if he didn't want to translate. Engin glared at him. Finally, he shot Kenan an angry look and, without words, demanded he translate. At last, Kenan did, looking apologetically at Mindy all the while.

"My name is Engin. I'd like to meet someone who knows my American friend, but I'm very upset about this diary. Why do missionaries come here for a few days and ruin things for us who live here? You obviously don't know what you're doing!"

Engin continued to vent his anger. His brow was damp with sweat. Hesitating, Kenan translated.

"My family is in jeopardy because of you. I could lose my job, and who knows what else. It's not like it is in your country here. We have to be careful. We have to hide."

Jeff wished Warren was there. Meanwhile, he reminded God of His promise to give wisdom when we ask. Then he asked. From somewhere deep inside, he dredged up a dose of courage.

"Sir," Jeff began. "We are very sorry. I don't blame you for being angry. I wish with all my heart this hadn't happened."

Kenan translated and Jeff continued.

"My sister is deeply hurt over this. She never intended to cause harm. This incident has reminded us of the seriousness of the situation in your country."

Jeff waited for the translation. Then he went on.

"Mindy wrote your name down only so we could greet you from your friend and because she wanted to pray for you every day."

At the last line, the man's face changed slightly. His anger seemed to subside a little. He raised his hands. "Listen. All I know is that Abdullah must have the diary, and he'll never quit harassing me. If I lose my job, I'll hold you all responsible."

Before Kenan finished translating, the man stormed off. Jeff held Mindy's hand when she started to cry. Stunned, everyone sat in silence.

Then Murat's eyes lit up. "I've got an older brother with some authority in the city. He's very open regarding my conversion. He's a good man and has some control with the police. I'll call him to see if he can track down that kid who took it. Then we'll know for sure."

Kenan smiled. "I'm not sure finding it will help. Engin seems very bitter. And from what I've seen of his temper, that may be his problem, not you or the diary."

The pastor nodded in agreement.

"But if the Brotherhood does have the diary..."

"Engin certainly has a point," Jeff concluded. He knew the team would have to talk with Warren about how to be more careful in these countries that were so different than America.

Later that evening, Jeff and the others arrived at Murat's house. Murat threw the door open to greet them. Smiling broadly, he brought his wife and daughter over to meet them.

"This is my wife, Nuray, and my daughter, Melis," he said proudly.

Jeff smiled at Nuray. A tiny Turkish woman with a broad smile, she fit perfectly under the crook of Murat's arm. Jeff was amazed at how closely her dark features and beautiful eyes were mirrored in her daughter's face.

Mindy had wrapped her favorite hair barrette for the ten-year-old, and Jeff smiled to see the two become instant friends. When Mindy put Melis' dark hair in a ponytail like her own, it seemed to swing with the beat of the music. The girl's eyes danced with excitement.

Balloons decorated the comfortable home. People filled every room. For a second, Jeff wondered whether the angry family members had come. But as he looked around, his attention was drawn to the ten-foot buffet table. K.J. had put down his camera and was already dishing up his plate.

Jeff snuck up behind him with a chuckle. "Hey, buddy. Just came to remind you not to drool in the food."

Hot pans were piled high with chicken and lamb. Rolls, salads and vegetables filled the table. Jeff saw a large, blue bowl filled with Turkish delight, the candy they'd sampled earlier. Another was filled with pistachio nuts, which Murat explained were called American peanuts in Turkey. In the center was a large cake decorated in several shades of pink.

But it was the traditional Turkish music that caught Jeff's greatest attention.

Murat and his wife kept busy talking to all the guests. It was a very festive time for them and the party-goers.

K.J. had asked permission to videotape the party. The only time he put the camera down was to stuff another bite in his mouth.

An hour later, Jeff was shocked when belly dancers appeared. He'd heard of them before, but now they were only a few feet away.

Mindy ran to his side. "Hey, Jeff," she said, giggling. "Why don't you try it?"

His face turned red. He shook his head and laughed nervously.

Melis was dancing with some other girls and two women. They had changed into clothes that looked more like scarves to Jeff.

Kenan appeared at Jeff's side. "What do you think?"

"Does everybody belly dance around here?"

Kenan laughed. "Yes. It's a big tradition. You'll find it everywhere. If you stayed here long, you would have to learn."

Jeff noticed Mindy giggling with Murat. They kept looking his direction. Then Murat stopped the music and made an announcement. Jeff wondered what was going on. Then he heard his name.

Kenan leaned closer to Jeff. "Murat has introduced you and the club as his special guests."

Jeff smiled. Everyone seemed to be looking at him.

Then Kenan doubled over with laughter.

"What's happening now?" Jeff begged.

"Murat says your sister has requested that you do a little belly dance."

Jeff felt blood rush to his head. For the second time that day, he had the urge to run.

"I forgot to tell you, Jeff," Kenan laughed. "It's a

tradition here to request a guest to belly dance. You don't want to offend your new friends, do you?"

Jeff shot an exasperated glance toward Mindy. She was laughing and clapping loudly for Jeff to come up. Everyone clapped. Louder and louder. K.J. was loving this.

Jeff knew he had no choice. The whole party stared. Finally, he forced his feet to take him to the small stage. Watching Melis and the other girls giggling, he decided to get into it.

Taking a deep breath, Jeff started moving his hips. Then he tried moving his stomach, but it didn't seem to work like the girls'. He felt so awkward and uncoordinated that he stopped completely.

Everyone applauded and whistled. Jeff saw K.J.'s camcorder zeroed in on his midriff. He realized everyone at home would see the tape. But since he couldn't get out of it, Jeff decided to make the best of it.

Taking Melis' hand, he started shaking his arms, then his back. The whole place erupted in applause.

Finally, Murat ran to the front. Pointing at Jeff, he got everyone to applaud even louder. Jeff took an exaggerated bow, dramatically threw his hands in the air, then walked off the stage, pointing to Mindy and K.J.

Everyone applauded wildly. Jeff took K.J.'s place behind the camera. Before long, the Reel Kids Club had learned to belly dance.

By 10:30, the guests had gone. Jeff and the others sat with Murat and Naray answering their questions about Christ. Even though Nuray wasn't ready to

accept Him as readily as Murat did, Jeff didn't think it would be long until she believed.

When it got late, Murat hugged everyone goodbye. Then he turned to Kenan. "Call me tomorrow. I'll let you know what my brother finds out about the diary."

Jeff knew God had used their visit to change a family's destiny.

Chapter 14

Arrested

As they leaned back against their seats on the bus, the team discussed the evening. Mindy cherished a beautiful gold candlestick Murat had given her. Everyone had gifts, but Mindy treasured hers the most.

"What are your plans for tomorrow?" Kenan wondered.

Jeff looked at the others. "We'd like to do some filming. But only if you think it's safe."

"Where would you like to go?" Kenan asked.

K.J. leaned over. "How about the Covered Bazaar? Mindy says it's one of the world's most fascinating markets, and I'd like to look for a gift for my mom. We also need footage of the Blue Mosque."

Jeff and Mindy exchanged nervous glances. "I think we'd all like to do some shopping," Jeff said, "but isn't the Blue Mosque close to where we ran into the Brotherhood?"

Kenan rubbed his chin. "You're right. It's not far from the park. But we'll be safer at the mosque since it has so many visitors."

Everyone nodded in agreement.

"It's settled, then," Kenan said. "You'll have to be careful with that camera, though, K.J. The Turkish government allows photography almost anywhere. But mosques are different. There are areas there where you are forbidden to even enter, let alone film."

"We'll be careful. Right, K.J.?" Jeff asked pointedly.

"I hope so," Mindy said. "I hope so."

Standing at the entrance to the Covered Bazaar, Jeff was ready for an exciting Monday—as long as they didn't run into the Brotherhood. Looking around, he couldn't believe how big the bazaar was.

"How far does it go?" he asked Kenan.

"I don't know exactly...an enormous area. It has over four thousand merchants."

"What's the secret to getting a good deal?" K.J. asked.

Kenan grinned. "They give the best deal to the first customer of the day. Since they believe in good luck, they make the first sale no matter how cheap it is."

The team looked at each other. This was good news!

"They even leave coins laying around for good luck," Kenan told them. "But watch out. They sell everything imaginable around here."

Jeff studied the maze of streets and tunnels filled with artfully displayed merchandise. K.J. filmed, while Mindy moved from merchant to merchant trying to bargain.

"What's this area called?" Jeff asked.

"Old Bedesten," Kenan replied. "It's one of the original areas of the city from the time of the Conquest. Some of the best goods in Turkey are sold here."

"Cool," Jeff said.

Jeff studied the area further. Brass and copper pots, pans and utensils were all arranged on tables. He saw things of every description, new and old, including ancient-looking swords and other weaponry. Antique coins, jewelry, costumes, pottery, and figurines were abundant.

"This is incredible," Jeff said, shaking his head in awe.

"Incredible," Mindy echoed, her brown eyes open wide. "I wish I could buy one of everything for Mom and Dad."

Jeff noticed her admiring a candlestick like the one Murat gave her. "How much is this?" she asked Kenan.

Kenan smiled. "Why don't you ask the man? The vendors speak a number of languages. Otherwise they wouldn't make much money."

Mindy turned to a short Turkish man with a printed turban wrapped around his head. "Sir. How much is this?"

The man grinned widely. "For you, only three hundred dollars."

Mindy thanked him and quickly put it back. "But it's nearly the same as the one Murat gave me! It's worth three hundred dollars? Wow!"

Deep in thought, Jeff picked up the candlestick. He remembered the book of Revelation talking about candlesticks. Each church was designed to be a light to the world, he had read. After staring at it for a few moments, he browsed along the maze of shopping tunnels. But he couldn't get the candlestick out of his mind.

Jeff looked at his watch. It was past noon. "We'd better head over to the Blue Mosque," he said to Kenan. "I don't know about you, but I could use an early night. All the stuff that's been happening is exhausting."

Kenan agreed. They rounded up Mindy and K.J., then found their way out of the bazaar.

"I'm almost out of money anyway," Mindy said, juggling her packages.

K.J. yawned, quickly covering his mouth.

Jeff laughed at him. "Looks like you're a little tired, too. All those extra things we hadn't planned are killin' us."

Kenan stifled a yawn himself. "Let's catch this red bus to the mosque," he directed. "It's only a few minutes from here."

As they arrived, Jeff craned his neck to look up at the massive structure. Kenan told them there were mosques like this all over the 10/40 region.

As they got closer, Jeff heard chanting. "We must have come at one of the five times Muslims pray every day," he observed.

Kenan nodded, knowing this was new to the team. "When I hear chanting," he confided, "it always makes me think about what prayer really is. I pray because I want to talk with God. Often. He's my Father, my Friend. He doesn't make me pray. It would be almost impossible not to pray, because I need Him."

The team nodded. They knew what Kenan meant.

"Do we need instructions before we go in?" Jeff asked, staring up at the mosque.

"Since there are lots of tourists here, we don't have to worry about the Brotherhood," Kenan answered. "But remember, there are places visitors can't go. And K.J., you can film inside, but no footage of anyone praying."

Trying to imitate a look his father sometimes gave him, Jeff shot K.J. a warning with his eyes. The others laughed. He wasn't very successful.

A shadow of seriousness crossed Kenan's face. "Let me know if you see a phone," he said. "I need to call Murat. We've got to put an end to this diary mystery."

They all agreed.

Looking around, Jeff wished he were standing in front of a church where people were praying in the name of Jesus. Remembering how God had reached Murat, Jeff prayed for all of the people inside the mosque.

He had to admit it was a beautiful building. A graceful cascade of domes and semi-domes filled his view. Six slender minarets pointed up from the corners of the building and the courtyard. The courtyard was as big as the mosque itself, with monumental entry ways at each of the three sides.

When K.J. had captured what he could on film, they headed inside. A technical design class Jeff was taking at school made him appreciate the amazing architecture and workmanship on the domes. He couldn't believe the exquisite colors.

The club members walked around for a few minutes. Kenan went to use the phone while K.J. filmed what he dared.

A while later, Kenan returned with a huge smile.

"You look like you have good news," Jeff commented.

"Great news! Murat's brother is amazing. His men found the kid this morning. With Mindy's backpack!"

Jeff was stunned.

"Not only that," Kenan said, "but he found out that the kid frequently stole things from tourists for the Brotherhood."

"Was the diary in the backpack?" Jeff asked.

"Yes. I guess the kid took the backpack and kept it for himself. He didn't even tell the Brotherhood. Murat's brother will meet us to return it tomorrow."

"Who knows?" Jeff said. "This could be the Lord's plan. Murat said his brother was open to hearing about the Gospel. Maybe we'll have a chance to talk with him." Jeff grinned. "Mindy will be so relieved. Let's go find them."

Mindy couldn't stop jumping up and down when she heard. "This means my diary had nothing to do with that man Engin's problems," she said happily.

When Mindy calmed down, they hurried to find

K.J. After ten minutes of searching, Jeff turned a corner. Suddenly, he gasped.

There was K.J.—surrounded by police.

Chapter 15

Deported

Jeff fought back panic. Then anger. He realized K.J. must have been caught filming in the wrong place. At that instant, Jeff wished he had kept a closer watch.

Kenan nearly ran into Jeff as he rounded the corner behind him. Jeff was frozen in place.

K.J. was sitting on the ground, handcuffed. His camera and bags were lined up like accomplices beside him.

"What shall we do?" Jeff asked desperately.

Kenan bit his lower lip. "Let's see what happened. It might be a mistake."

By then, Mindy had seen the situation. She tapped her foot like she was ready to explode. Jeff and Kenan hurried over to K.J. Mindy's foot was still working, but she wasn't going anywhere.

Suddenly, Jeff saw what was happening. Abdullah and an angry swarm of Brotherhood were walking their direction. Jeff and Kenan stopped in their tracks. Jeff felt trapped.

"There's the others! Arrest them, too," Abdullah cried.

Jeff was stunned. Trembling, he pulled his shoulders back and stood as tall as he could. Abdullah strutted over to him. Surrounded by police now, Jeff and Kenan were quickly handcuffed. Then Mindy.

"Hey," Jeff protested loudly, fighting rising fear. "What's this all about? We didn't do anything."

Abdullah laughed out loud. Turning to the police, he spoke boldly in clear English. "These are the ones we've been telling you about. They have broken our laws from the day they arrived. They've been filming things they shouldn't."

Jeff was speechless. Even though he was sitting, K.J. was shaking like a leaf. Mindy was scared and mad. It had been against her better judgment to come to the mosque, but she hadn't said anything to the others. She was tired of always being the one worrying.

Kenan was trying to reason with the police captain. But Jeff could see that the captain was as angry as Abdullah and his men. Jeff was confused. Was this K.J.'s fault? Or were the police on the side of the Brotherhood? Had the Brotherhood finally played their trump card?

Kenan turned sadly to Jeff. "This time, there is nothing I can do. We're going to jail."

The words stung. The good news about the diary was forgotten. After a few minutes, they were herded outside and into the police wagon like cattle.

Jeff had never seen the inside of a police wagon, but it was like he had imagined. Cramped. Dirty. And as smelly as an outhouse.

As the policeman drove over the pitted streets and screeched around corners, the team bounced into each other. Mindy was huddled in the corner, bravely trying to keep from crying. But this was too much. All at once, tears streamed from her eyes.

"Mindy," Jeff said gruffly, "that is not going to help. God is the only one who can help. Pray."

Jeff heard his own words, but he didn't feel that way. He felt like crying with her. At that moment, he didn't see how God *could* help them. But just then, Murat and the miracle of his conversion popped into Jeff's mind. He remembered how God had changed him. *God is powerful,* Jeff told himself. *God is powerful.*

Moments later, the wagon screeched to a stop. The team was pushed into an empty room at the police station.

After a while, a police captain entered, speaking at full volume. "I hear you were warned a few days ago to stop propagating your religious beliefs. And yet you have continued."

Jeff watched carefully, his head down.

Kenan began to say something but was cut off. "Be quiet," the captain snarled. "I've had enough. We've been watching you. We know you've been bringing in teams for a long time."

Jeff saw Kenan's back stiffen and his head come up. "Sir, in our constitution, there is complete freedom of religion. I demand to see a lawyer."

The captain's laugh was hollow. "A lawyer! You're going to need more than that."

Jeff wondered what that meant.

The captain went on. "Abdullah has given us detailed reports of your activities this week. He's always looking out for the good of our country."

"His reports are lies!" Kenan cried. "The Brotherhood doesn't represent the views of the Turkish people."

The captain's eyes narrowed dangerously.

"They represent my views. Right now that's all that matters."

Jeff got the picture. The captain was one of the Brotherhood himself. Remembering Kenan's words about it all depending on the police captain, he knew they were in trouble. This one wasn't a good man.

The captain looked them over with contempt. "We're going to take harsh measures to put an end to your activities."

"What measures?" Mindy cried, terror filling her eyes.

"You'll see," the captain said, storming out of the room.

Jeff and the others were left alone, with two policemen guarding the door.

"What do we do now?" Mindy asked worriedly.

"I don't know," Kenan said. "If I could just call Parmelee."

"In America," K.J. said, "you're allowed one phone call. What about here?"

"Like I told you before," Kenan said with a nervous chuckle, "it all depends on the police captain."

"Won't he get in trouble if he makes bad judgments?" Jeff reasoned.

"Maybe," Kenan said. "But it looks like he's been doing this for a long time. He's definitely in charge here."

An hour passed. The captain finally returned. "How is my little band of Christians now?"

Jeff rolled his eyes. "Can't we take these handcuffs off?" he asked. "We're not common criminals."

The captain gave him a snide look. "Soon enough."

Jeff wondered what he was trying to say.

The captain looked at Jeff. "Where is the American man who was with you earlier?"

"You mean Mr. Russell? He's at Kenan's house recovering from a broken leg."

"Too bad," the captain snickered. Then he looked at Kenan. "What about your wife?"

Kenan looked up. "She's at home. I'd like to call her."

"You can call her. In fact, that's a good idea. I have also contacted our immigration office. You'll all be leaving soon."

"What do you mean?" Jeff asked.

The captain stared Jeff in the eye until he turned away. "You're all being deported. Tonight."

Chapter 16

The Missing Candlestick

Jeff didn't want to believe what he had heard. Mindy's jaw clenched.

"We all have visas," Kenan said. "You can't do this."

"You mean you all *had* visas. We're putting you on a plane for Frankfurt, Germany at nine o'clock."

The captain turned to Kenan. "Go ahead and call home. And make it fast. Tell your wife to pack her things. A police car will be there to pick her up within the hour."

Then the captain's eye locked on Jeff. "Your friend...

Russell, is it? He'll be under house arrest until he has recovered sufficiently to travel. Then he'll be sent home too."

Jeff was stunned.

The captain laughed again. "That's all."

Surrounded by police, Jeff felt like all the energy had drained out of his body. He wondered why God was allowing their mission to end so soon.

He'd been so humiliated when they were rushed to the airport in that awful police wagon. They hadn't even had a chance to pick up their luggage. It would be sent later, the captain said. Worst of all, the video would never be finished. They were leaving a week earlier than they had planned.

Jeff had always prided himself on taking care of his little sister, even if she didn't always need his help. Now she sat alone while he wallowed in his own problems. He felt like he'd let everyone down.

Kenan sat quietly, looking like his world had come to an end. Jeff felt helplessly responsible. Listening to the continual airport announcements, he sat with the others. Despairing. Watching the clock.

It was almost eight. Jeff saw Murat and Parmelee headed their way. When he saw that they too were surrounded by police, his heart sank. Not only were Kenan and Parmelee being deported, but Murat too!

Looking closer, he saw no handcuffs. Why was Murat grinning from ear to ear?

When Kenan spotted them, he jumped from his seat. "Why are you guys smiling?" he cried in disbelief.

Parmelee's beautiful smile radiated at her husband. "God has done a miracle!"

Jeff leaned forward. Parmelee spoke in a rush of excitement.

"After receiving the call from Kenan, I phoned Murat," she explained. "He called his brother, who has been investigating the Brotherhood for a while now. Apparently, many visitors have complained over the last few months."

Jeff couldn't believe what he was hearing. Parmelee went on.

"His brother worked to get the deportation orders reversed, but by the time he succeeded, they had already taken you to the airport."

"What else?" Jeff asked.

"We're all free to stay!"

At first, the team was too stunned to speak. Then everyone rejoiced together. Parmelee had to stop everyone to finish her story.

"The police captain is in serious trouble," she reported. "The Brotherhood's been warned. They'll be watched closely from now on and arrested if they continue to harass people. The Turkish government does not support their tactics."

Jeff was stunned.

"The only thing we might not get back is our literature," she said. "It appears that Abdullah convinced the policemen to let him destroy it."

Kenan didn't look upset. "If God has reversed the deportation orders, He'll help us get new literature too."

The team nodded, thankful for their friend's faith.

Jeff spoke quietly. "I shouldn't have been angry at Abdullah either. I should have prayed that he'd come back to the truth."

"We still can, Jeff," Mindy pointed out. "Maybe that's some of the good that can come out of this—us knowing that he needs prayers."

Parmelee smiled at Mindy. "There's another good thing that God has brought from all our troubles."

"What's that?"

"The kid who took your diary had a friend who knew English read some of it to him."

Mindy turned red. "No!"

"It's okay," Parmelee assured her. "He was so impressed by your love for God that he wants to meet you to apologize for taking it."

With her mouth wide open, Mindy plopped onto the bench beside Jeff.

In silence, the team watched a jet take off, climbing higher and higher. Quickly, it was out of sight. Tears of joy slipped down their faces. As usual, K.J. was planning how he was going to shoot the scene.

Jeff's heart was filled with worship to God. It was because of His power that they would have another week to do His work in this incredible city. Jeff looked around at his new friends. When his eyes rested on Murat, he thought of the candlestick he had given Mindy. He realized that the candlestick of the early church had been missing for a long time.

But Jeff knew Jesus was lighting another one in Turkey.

One that might light up the entire 10/40 window.